Extinction Pulse Copy

Nightfall: Book One

Kevin Partner

Scribbleit

Contents

1. Elijah   1

2. Elijah   10

3. Elijah   19

4. Grace   28

5. Hannah   38

6. Hannah   47

7. Abby & Rae   56

8. Samuel & Ruth   65

9. Elijah   76

10. Hannah   86

11. Abby & Rae   96

12. Abby & Rae   105

13. Grace   117

14. Elijah   126

15. Hannah   133

16. Abby & Rae   144

17. Abby & Rae   155

18. Samuel & Ruth   168

19. Elijah   176

20. Elijah   185

21. Elijah   193

22. Elijah   204

23. Elijah   211

24. Grace   219

Epilogue   227

Author's Note   231

Free Story and More from Me   233

Elijah

Day 1: Glendale, CA.

Detective Elijah Wade glanced up at the colorful streaks of light dancing in the evening sky as he hit the back of a line of traffic. He pulled a cigarette out of its red packet, lit it with practiced ease, and leaned on the horn.

Time and again his eyes flicked upwards, squinting as his focus shifted from the blinding red and white lights of the traffic around him to the gentler, but more ominous hues looming over the towering city buildings. There was something about them that creeped him out. He ran his hand down the back of his neck, smoothing out the goosebumps.

He shifted his gaze back to the line of vehicles. Two hours before his flight and decades of experience in Glendale, CA traffic told him he wouldn't make it. He'd spent all day at his desk poring over evidence sheets and witness statements, getting nowhere. And, because of that he'd left for the airport too late.

But he *couldn't* miss the flight. His eighteen-year-old daughter was having heart surgery in New York, and he was waiting for a call with news from her mother. He touched the star pendant that hung around his neck. She'd given it to him ten years ago and wouldn't know that he'd kept it on him every day since.

He shook his head, grunting with frustration. He was her father. He *had* to be there for the operation. But he was also a detective working a case — multiple homicide. More would follow if they didn't catch the killer.

So, he'd said he'd arrive for when she woke up, and *that* promise was now sailing into the sunset to rot with all the others.

And *what* a sunset. Between the tower blocks, he could see a deep red spreading from the west, like blood staining cloth. Above it, the sky brooded orange as if the heavens were on fire.

His cell brought him back to earth.

"Wade."

"Lige, we've got him!"

He recognized his partner's voice. "Who?"

"The serial killer - the Cleaner!"

Now he was all attention, though his eyes remained on the sky.

"What? How?"

He heard Terry Nugent chuckle.

"You added those plates to the system, remember? We got lucky: patrol ran them on a mini-van and pulled him over. Double lucky, because it was Oscar. Twenty years' experience — that guy's got a nose for it."

"Cut to the chase, brother."

"Sorry. Oscar checked his driver's I.D., and it was fake. As he was getting the perp out of the car, his partner found a black bag with blood-stained clothes in it. And they found his real I.D."

"Jeez." Wade felt that familiar sickness. The mix of triumph and disappointment when all their efforts to find the girl alive looked like they were in vain.

"But look, Lige, I'm only telling you because I knew you'd go all crazy on me if I didn't. You get yourself on that plane — you need to be with Kelly."

Wade's hand hovered over the switch that would set off the berries and cherries.

"Was it one of the suspects?"

"No. Out of the blue. But Oscar's sure it's our man. Unless there's two serial killers on the loose. Name's Silas Lynch."

"All that work and we were barking up the wrong tree. Where have you put him?"

"He's in the tank. Oscar couldn't get nothin' out of him, so I'm heading there now. Says he wants his lawyer."

"I bet he does."

"Claims the blood is his. Says the girl ain't dead. Hey, Lige. You seen the sky?"

The car to his left honked at him as Wade involuntarily tugged on the steering wheel. Was it possible? Becky Powell had been missing for over a week, the latest of a series of lost girls across the state, all of whom had eventually turned up dead — dumped in black bags on the side of the road. The chief had been forced to call in the help of LA's homicide division, but if a Glendale patrol had caught the monster, then he was going to be damned if he'd let members of his former department question him. This was *Elijah's* case.

"I'm coming in," he said, cutting Terry off mid-protest. He liked his partner but didn't trust him to get what they needed from this Lynch character, or to hold off Homicide once they learned of the arrest.

He flicked on his lights, tossed the half-finished smoke out the window, took a right and swung the car around, heading downtown and into the eye of the storm.

Glancing at his cell when it rang again, his stomach lurched.

"Lyndsey! Is Kelly okay?"

"She's in recovery. The surgeon says the operation went well, but they won't know for sure for a couple of days."

"Thank God." Well, that was at least one weight off his shoulders.

"Is your flight on time? I can come meet you—she'll be kept under for a while."

Wade paused, trying to come up with the right words as his eyes strayed to the star pendant that hung from his mirror.

"You're not coming, are you?"

"Lyndsey, we've just arrested a suspected serial killer. We think he's taken a local girl. She might be alive."

"Jesus, Elijah! Your own daughter is fighting for her life! Your place is here! Don't let her down again."

He couldn't find anything to say.

"Message received, you son of a b—"

The line went dead.

By the time he arrived at the department building, he had to push his way through a crowd of officers and bystanders, all looking up at the sky, ignoring the even more gaudy festive lights adorning the police station. He glanced up briefly. He'd seen the aurora australis once on a trip to southern Chile, but this beat that, hands down. The familiar green pulsing bands were there—brighter than he'd ever seen—but they'd been joined by every color in the visible spectrum. It was as if God had spilled his paints across the heavens.

And there was an eerie whistling sound in the still air.

He paused for a moment, caught between wonder and an unquantifiable feeling of dread. He had a vision, as the people stood looking up, of moths around a flame. There was a tension about the crowd. He didn't like it at all.

"Elijah!"

He snapped out of it and turned to see Terry at the door.

"Who's on the desk? Hey, you look like crap."

"I'm okay, just beat. It's Joe's shift. Don't worry, I've told him to slow walk it."

Good. That was code for taking as long as possible to inform their Homicide partners. It ought to buy a couple of hours of interrogation time.

Wade ran past the public area and swiped his ID. No luck. Cursing, he waved at a figure on the other side who opened it manually, before half-running toward the holding pen.

"Ah want to see my lawyer."

The 'pen' was a tiny cell made up of whitewashed cinder block on three sides and bars on the fourth. It was where they kept the most dangerous suspects.

A man stood, gripping the bars. "Ah said, Ah want my lawyer."

The first thing Wade noticed was what a good-looking man Lynch was. The second thing was the dried blood under his fingernails.

"And Ah want to wash my hands." There was a trace of the Mississippi about his accent.

Wade heard Terry's Hush Puppies on the concrete floor. Then another voice called out. "Detective Nugent."

"Hey, Sarge," Terry responded, speaking into a doorway along the corridor.

"We could do with your help. Crowd control. Might be best if you put your uniform on. I can't raise anyone on this piece of junk, and I need someone with brains and composure out there. That's why I'm not sending Detective Wade."

Nugent sighed, but acknowledged the sergeant, then glanced at Elijah before shrugging and heading off.

Wade leaned back to shout along the corridor. "Joe, I'm going to interview Lynch. Will you sit in with me?"

"No can do, Detective, sorry. We got a four-fifteen situation developing outside and I need every boot on the ground." DeSantos's bald head poked around the door frame.

"What's going on out there?"

The sergeant shrugged. "I'm getting reports of fist fights and general aggravation. It's something about the sky. Didn't you see it when you came in?"

"Looks like an aurora. Spectacular, but I don't see why that would cause trouble."

"I don't know. I'm calling in the cavalry, if I can get hold of them. Cell network is patchy. Hey, what's that?"

The sound of running boots echoed along the corridor and Wade joined DeSantos as he jogged back to the door dividing the public and back-office areas.

"Sarge! We got trouble."

DeSantos glanced at Wade, nodded, and then pulled the door open. A dozen people had piled into the outer area, and others were trying to get inside, pushing and shoving as the room filled with groans. Some people fell to the floor. Wade saw the clothes of one of them smoking, and the smell of... what was it? It reminded him of warm summer days. Barbeque? He swallowed his disgust as DeSantos pulled a young patrol officer behind the desk.

"What's going on, Riley?"

"Radio not working. Me, Tubbs and Chen tried to hold the door, but... Sarge, I... I don't feel great..."

Wade took Riley's shoulders and opened the door to the back-office, pushing him through. "Get hold of CDU, okay?"

He turned back to stand beside the sergeant. "Help may be a while coming, Joe."

DeSantos nodded as a Latina man pushed his way to the front.

"Hey, I'm burnin' up, man! And I can't see right. It's like I got those lights floatin' in front of my eyeballs. I need to go to ER, stat!"

"Stand back," DeSantos said, then he raised his hand and yelled "Quiet!"

The people crowding into the station only noticed when Wade joined in. "Everyone out!" He took his 1911 and pointed it at the ceiling.

The room filled with cries of alarm and protest, but Wade simply pointed at the door. "Get out onto the sidewalk and then we'll let you in one at a time. This isn't Beirut!"

A patrol officer pushed the door open and stood back as people surged out, muttering to each other. But rather than waiting out there, they dispersed onto the streets. If Wade was any judge, more than half of them were looking for trouble. The last man to go called out, "I'm sick, you b—" before the officer slammed the door behind him.

"Jeez, what in hell's name is going on?" Wade said, his daughter, wife and the suspected serial killer in the tank all forgotten as he peered through the toughened glass.

"Keep back," the officer said. "There's something bad going down. It's like my blood's made of liquid fire."

Wade blinked at the man. "Jenkins, isn't it? What happened out there?"

The young patrol officer wiped his forehead, and Wade half imagined the skin would come off with his hand it looked so gray and lifeless. "They started gathering as the sun went down. Those lights in the sky, they were amazing... And that sound. Like someone chanting..."

For a moment, Jenkins's eyes glazed over, as if he'd been hypnotized.

"Then what, officer?"

"Oh, sorry. Some old woman started calling out, saying her eyes were burning. Then more and more of them. A couple — they held their hands up. They wanted God to lift them up to the sky. Man, it was... it was surre—"

Wade caught him as he slumped, dragging him across the floor to lean him against the wall.

Then Terry Nugent staggered through the door and Wade left the patrol officer to help his partner.

"Jeez, brother," he said, kicking the front door shut behind him and helping him to a chair.

Wade kneeled beside his partner, but his eye was caught by the scene beyond as he looked through the glass of the station door at the sky. The colors had been bright before, but now they were livid, pulsing as if alive, and he imagined he could feel heat coming off them.

"Come on Terry, let's get you out back." He helped Nugent to his feet, draping his partner's arms around his shoulder. He looked over at the sergeant. "Have you called an ambulance?"

"Lines aren't working."

Wade pulled the inner door open. "Then I don't have any more answers, Joe. We'll have to wait for the cavalry to arrive."

"But what's going on? What's making them sick?"

"I don't know, but it's got something to do with those lights in the sky. My guess? Radiation. But I'm going to take Terry inside, find somewhere for him to rest up. Then we'll get Jenkins."

By the time Elijah was making his way back to the front desk, DeSantos was half-dragging the young police officer toward the open door.

"I don't understand how he got so sick so fast," the sergeant said. "I mean, if it was the lights, they've only been out for a couple of hours."

Wade took Jenkins's other arm. "I don't know. Has he been on patrol today?"

"Yeah. Six hours street work."

Grimacing, Wade helped the officer into a seat in the small office that served as kitchen and sick bay. He had a nasty feeling. A real nasty feeling.

"Rich, can you hear me?"

"Yeah."

"When did you start feeling bad — was it before the lights appeared in the sky?"

The officer nodded. "Been creeping up on me all day. Figured I was... coming down with something..."

"What are you thinking?" DeSantos asked as he and Wade got to their feet.

"That whatever is causing the aurora has been doing it for hours without anyone noticing because it was daytime. Have you been out much today?"

The sergeant shook his head.

"Me neither. But Terry's been working the cleaner case, and he's got it bad."

"You think it's an attack? Nukes?"

"Can't be ICBMs or we'd know it."

"A dirty bomb?"

"Maybe, but that wouldn't explain the lights. Look, Joe, try to get hold of anyone from headquarters, will you? I'm going to check on our prisoner."

Wade left the sergeant, said some words of comfort to his partner and the police officer as they sat, slumped, in their chairs, and walked toward the tank.

Lynch was waiting for him.

"What's going on? I'm still waiting for my lawyer, and I want to clean myself up."

"You got no right to demand anything," Wade said.

"I got every right. I know the law, and you can't talk to me without my lawyer, unless you intend to charge me, in which case I'll be takin' the fifth until you do."

Wade stabbed a finger at him. "Now you listen to me, you piece of filth. I haven't got time to waste on scum like you right now, so just sit tight and we'll get to you when we get to you. But if you want anything from me, you'll tell me right now where Becky Powell is."

"Filth?" Lynch sneered. "Fine words coming from you, Detective Wade. Your hands are dirtier than mine, by all accounts. And I never heard of Becky Powell."

Wade swung away from the suspect. The man was too valuable to them for Wade to lose him to an accusation of police brutality. He marched along the corridor, boots echoing on the polished floor then, as he pulled on the door, a thought hit him between the eyes and sent a chill through his soul.

How did Lynch know his name?

And then the lights went out.

2

Elijah

Wade thrust his hand up to fend off the bright flashlight shining at him. "Joe?"

"It's me. C'mon, let's get out of here."

"Hey! Don't you leave me here on my own in the dark!" Lynch called out.

Wade made his way back to the sergeant's office and quickly found a flashlight on a rack beside the desk. He flicked it on and marched back to the pen, holding it up outside the cell bars. "You want some light? Tell me where Rebecca is, and you can have this one. It's fully charged, and we'll be back long before it runs out."

Wade pointed the flashlight into Lynch's face and watched him closely. There it was! A brief look at the ceiling as the suspect thought through his options. Lynch *was* the killer, and he was considering whether to fess up, or deny it and stay in the dark.

"I'll sue your ass if you leave me here!"

Withdrawing the flashlight, Wade turned away. "Suit yourself." Now he knew they'd gotten their man; he also knew where to start looking.

He and DeSantos made their way back to the main door, having stopped off at the break room to give Terry Nugent a flashlight. The other officer was unconscious.

A weird silence wrapped around the dark public area as Wade emerged. Beyond the front entrance, he could glimpse the occasional handheld light moving, and it took him a moment to realize what was wrong with this picture. "What's happened to the cars?"

"Yeah. I mean, have they all gone?"

"I don't think so," Wade said, moving up to the glass and looking into the darkness. "They're there, but their lights are off. Jeez, you reckon it's an EMP?"

DeSantos shrugged. "Sure starting to sound like a nuke, isn't it?"

"Even the sky's gone dark," Wade said, pointing into the sky. "Except for the stars."

A squawk from his hip, and Wade grabbed at his radio.

"This is the chief to all units. A state of emergency has been declared. You are ordered to return to your department and equip yourselves against chemical agents. Render all possible aid to civilians, but otherwise, for now, hunker down. More to follow. Chief out."

The two officers looked at each other.

"State of emergency?" DeSantos said, shaking his head. "Maybe we were right, maybe it is an attack."

Wade shrugged. "Can you get me Lynch's possessions? Car keys, driver's license? And a mask?"

"Sure. Why?"

"I think Becky Powell is alive. I'm going to go find her."

"Are you serious? Didn't you hear what the chief said? Jeez, Elijah, aren't you in enough trouble?"

Slapping the sergeant on the shoulders, Wade said, "No choice. We don't know what's going to happen next, and she'll have been tied up. She'll die if I don't go."

"You want me to come?"

"No. You need to look after Terry, Jenkins and Lynch. I'll be as quick as I can, and I'll bring supplies. Sound good?"

"Whatever you say, Elijah."

"You're the ranking officer, you give the orders."

Joe DeSantos gave a grim chuckle and shook his head. "I've got a feeling that doesn't mean much at the moment. I'll go get Lynch's things."

Wade smiled, trying to offer reassurance he didn't feel, then returned to the window and looked out. Some of the streetlights had failed, but he could see that people were still out there and, beyond, he noticed that the usual flow of passing headlights had stopped, leaving just a few lights that looked, from here, as if they weren't moving. Was it an EMP? On the face of it, that made some sort of weird sense — there had to be a connection between the lights in the sky and the power outage. And what about the fights that had broken out? Was it just opportunism?

He shook his head — he didn't have enough to go on to solve the mystery, so he focused on the one thing he could do — give this young girl a chance. And, with that thought, his mind switched to the New York hospital that was treating his daughter, Kelly. Had they lost power, too? Jeez, what if she was on life support?

But there was nothing he could do from here. He couldn't help Kelly right now, but he could go after Becky. So, he would.

Wade ran into the open, leaving the police department building behind him and clutching his Colt while he scanned the area, glad that the darkness hid his appearance as he made his way through familiar backstreets. He'd learned a lot about Becky Powell while working on the case. She was no paragon of virtue, but she didn't deserve to be left forgotten in her abductor's apartment while the city responded to... whatever was happening.

The last streetlight had flickered out as he'd shut the door of the station, and he could hear the unmistakable sounds of fear and insurrection in the distance. Shattering glass, shouts and far-off gunshots. But nothing mechanical and no police sirens. It was as if someone had turned off civilization. Despite his focus on Becky, he could sense the cogs in his mind turning in the background. What was going on? Were they under attack? What was the chief going to do about it? The police couldn't hide in their department buildings if the city was coming apart, could they?

Stop this! Focus, Elijah.

Looking up for a moment, he saw that the aurora had faded or, perhaps, gone behind a bank of cloud. Somehow, he felt better for that.

He considered the best route to take. According to his driver's license, Lynch lived in an apartment block near Fremont Park, Glendale. Under normal circumstances, Wade would head north along Brand Boulevard, but his instinct told him to use the quieter roads, so he ran past the city jail and then cut across to North Jackson Street, his weapon following the line of his flashlight as he jogged through the unfamiliar darkness. He'd never known the city like this—devoid of the sounds of vehicles moving, music playing and, above all, the hum of people talking and walking, except for the occasional sudden sounds of violence in the distance.

He ran up the middle of the road, head moving from side to side, skirting around cars that, it seemed, had stopped in their tracks. People gathered around them, coalescing into groups, talking in hurried whispers, flashlights sweeping from one to the other, scuffles in the darkness Most seemed to be waiting for the authorities to come to their aid, some lay leaning against their tires, a few being actively tended, others left, ignored in the chaos. Many wore masks — the sort they kept in their gloveboxes.

Then, above the hubbub of frightened people, and the slapping of his boots on the road, he heard something else, something that chilled his blood and made him stop.

A woman stood beside a red Toyota, a cell phone held to her ear, looking up with her mouth open.

Wade looked around. He thought, at first, that she was looking at the moon, which had just risen over the horizon, giving a washed out, but welcome light.

Then he saw it. Black against the dark sky, obscuring the stars as it went, its huge shape faintly lit from one side.

A plane. A massive plane.

Wade grabbed the woman by the hand. "Come on! Run!"

She unfroze and, as he ran, he heard screams going up and the patter of feet behind him. He was the Pied Piper, but whether he was leading them to safety or destruction, he had no idea.

It sounded like something out of a war movie — the whining cry of a dying bird heading straight down. All he could think of was running, even though, for all he knew, he could be heading straight for it. But he was sure as hell not going to die standing still. So, he pulled the woman with him, even as she screamed, shouted and stumbled, her shoes flying off.

As they made it to the intersection with East Doran, the noise in the sky above them reached an ear-splitting peak. They had seconds left as, behind them, people shrieked, their footsteps swallowed up in the roar. In that instant, he spotted an underground garage with its door open, and, with a final effort, he pulled the woman toward it even as the air around them exploded like a blast furnace. He felt the heat searing the back of his legs as he pushed her inside and threw himself in after her. He wrapped his arms around the woman, gasping as the garage filled with scorching heat and overwhelming noise.

Then, when he thought he couldn't bear it any longer, it was gone.

He let her go and slowly turned around.

The garage entrance was the picture-frame around a view of hell.

He gagged as an acrid stench burned the inside of his nose, roasting his lungs and making his eyes stream. He could barely take in enough air to remain on his feet, but he wasn't thinking of that as he gazed out on a burning world.

They stood there — Wade and the nameless woman — saying nothing, as they took in the leaping flames and roiling black smoke. Nothing moved, nothing survived.

How long did they remain there, looking out on this vision of hell? It might have been ten minutes, or perhaps an hour as, slowly, the flames died down a little. But he finally became aware that his lungs were straining to bring in fresh oxygen through the arid air.

"We've gotta get out," he said. "We'll suffocate in here."

She nodded and allowed him to guide her toward the front of the garage.

Shielding his face with his arm, Wade tried to make sense of what he was seeing now they were out in the open. The night had been banished to be replaced with bright orange flames, wreathed in pulsing tendrils of black smoke that reached for the dark sky. Among the flames were the tortured carcasses of cars, trucks and other things he couldn't make out. He couldn't see the main fuselage, so the plane hadn't come down on top of them, and he guessed it must have landed back the way they'd come, vomiting ignited aviation fuel that consumed everything, and everyone, it touched. And it was sucking the oxygen out of their hiding place.

"Come on," he said.

"Where?"

He gestured along the street. "That way. We've got to get ahead of the flames."

She nodded, then gripped his hand. "I'm Laura. Thank you for saving me."

"I'm Elijah, and you're welcome. Come on, let's go."

He led her out of the garage and into the inferno. He smelled burning hair and realized it was his own, and felt her resist, but pushed through. To go back was to die.

They were funneled along by the solid row of apartment buildings, and he took them beneath a stand of palm trees, lit up like beacons, until, finally, they reached a side road and could escape from the heat behind a commercial building.

He leaned back against the building's cool brickwork, then immediately flinched as pain seared through him.

"Your coat's smoking," she said, helping him to take it off. It fell away, the fresh wind easing his pain, and he stood there self-consciously aware that she was examining his naked back. "I'm not a doctor, but that looks pretty sore. We'd better find a hospital."

He turned to face her. "They've got enough to worry about, and there's something I've got to do."

She was about to speak when a flashing blue light caught his eye. It was farther along the main street, away from the plane wreck.

"Come on," Wade said. "Let's get out of here."

He pulled the badge and wallet out of his jacket and slid them into his singed slacks. "Shame, that was my favorite."

"It saved your life," she said. "And you saved mine."

He always felt uncomfortable with lavish gratitude. After all, he'd just been doing his job, just doing what anyone would.

They walked past the intersection and toward the row of blue and red flashing lights. *Thank God*, he thought. This was the first evidence he'd seen of any response by the emergency services. At least someone was taking action.

The young firefighter on the other side of the cordon stood aside to let them through. "Head over to the triage station," he said, through his heavy mask, waving behind him where a group in fire department, police and hospital uniforms were gathered around an ambulance. The constant flicking of the battery-powered emergency lights gave the scene an even more chaotic feel, and he was glad when they left the cordon behind.

"Good grief, you didn't come out of that alive, did you?"

A masked police officer Wade didn't recognize looked them up and down with his flashlight.

"By the skin of our teeth. What's the situation, officer?"

The cop shrugged and shook his head. "Seems to me it's the end of the world. The end of the f—"

"My name's Detective Elijah Wade, Glendale P.D." He flashed his badge, noting the surprise in the young officer's expression. Wade gestured at his bare torso and managed a smile. "I appreciate this isn't regulation uniform."

The officer nodded. "Yes, Detective."

"Now, what do you know?"

"Not much. Comms went down an hour ago, but we'd gotten a request to provide support to ER at Memorial— folks turning up with burns and sickness. The lights. You saw them?"

"I saw them. Go on."

"Then the power went out, and the chief sent us onto the streets to keep order. Put a curfew in place. When the plane came down, we wound up here. Seems like a terrorist attack to me. You think?"

"Your guess is as good as mine, brother. Now, will you look after this lady?"

"Sure, I'll get her inside and have a medic look over her."

"You will not!" she snapped before turning to Wade. "You're the one who needs to see a doctor, not me."

"I'm fine. I've got a job to do."

"What sort of job?"

"I'm working a case."

Her jaw dropped open. "What? Can't you see what's going on around us?"

"Sure I can, but someone's depending on me."

He could sense *what about me?* forming in her mind, but she swallowed it, and that show of strength made it easier. "You don't need me, Laura. Get yourself checked over and then..."

"And then what?"

He shrugged. "Search me. I guess we'll have to see how it plays out, but I gotta go. This is what I have to do."

She looked at him for a moment, then hugged him and, without another word, headed toward the ambulance.

"Does that thing work?" Wade asked the officer.

"Some of the equipment does, but we had to push the ambulance here. No one's getting a ride any time soon. This case you're working, must be a big one."

Wade nodded. "Serial killer. I've got a lead on where he might have stashed a woman."

"Alive?"

"Maybe."

The officer nodded. "Wait here a sec." He headed into the group of people tending the injured, then returned a few seconds later. "Best I can do," he said, handing over a blue jacket with Glendale Memorial Hospital stamped on the back.

"Thanks. Keep safe," Wade said. He took his bearings and then headed past the cordon, saying a silent prayer that, after all this death and destruction, he'd find Becky Powell alive.

3

Elijah

Wade looked out over Ventura Freeway from the North Jackson Street road bridge. In the west, the sky glowed amber with a smoke-blurred haze that wrapped around the towers, consuming the Chase Bank building. Others lined the bridge on either side, all gazing at the destruction, whispering as if they were beside a death bed. He could hear sirens in the distance, but no other sign of the response of emergency services.

He stood there in frozen disbelief. How many planes had come down over the city? He knew that LAX was one of the busiest airports in the country, but he didn't have any idea how many planes would be in the sky above the city at any one time. It must have been dozens, surely? And if the outage that had taken out Glendale had been something like an EMP — which seemed likely given that it had knocked out the city's vehicles and communications — then what would that do to air traffic?

Knock it out of the sky.

Jeez. What if that's happened across the country? He'd seen the direct effects on the human body of the radiation — or whatever it was — given off by the lights, but it also seemed to have taken down the infrastructure that fed and maintained humanity, while simultaneously killing thousands of air travelers. Poor devils to be in the air when this happened.

What if New York City was burning like this? How could Kelly survive? Terror flooded his gut. He couldn't begin to comprehend the scale of it. He leaned back, holding onto

the safety fence and rocking on his heels, then looked up at
the sky. Where had the aurora come from? Would it come
back?

If the same had happened across the country and all
vehicles had stopped, then how would he even get to New
York? But he had to go. He *had* to. Whatever it took. This
time he wouldn't let Kelly down. She would have been
inside the hospital while the lights were in the sky, and he
suspected the same would be true of his ex-wife. She'd have
been beside Kelly's bed. He should have been next to her.

But, of course, it had never been quite that simple. His
life and his job were both here, and it had been Lindsay's
choice to relocate on the other side of the country when she
and Wade split up. None of that quelled the guilt that was
threatening to overwhelm him. A father's job is to protect
his children, come what may. And he would go to her or die
in the attempt.

He realized, as he watched the skies, that if he'd been on
the plane as promised, he'd have fallen from the sky with all
the other thousands of passengers who'd died tonight. That
broken promise had saved his life. Now he was ready to risk
everything in its fulfilment.

How far was it to New York? A couple thousand miles.
That would take a long time by foot. He'd have to find
another way. He'd been in the Air Force special services, but
he'd seen what had happened to planes in the air. What
about those on the ground? What about older airplanes that
didn't have the same degree of electronics? An old Cessna
172, perhaps?

But before he could go, he had business here. It was odd
how, after working on a missing person case, you developed
a closeness to the victim. He'd never met her but having
spent so much time reading the testimony of friends and
family, looking at her photos and the handbag found at the
scene of the abduction, he felt he knew her. And right now,

he was her only hope. Kelly had her mother with her, Becky had no one.

So, he decided to keep his focus on the one soul he *might* be able to save and work out how to cross a continent tomorrow.

Wade left the other bystanders there as they watched the city die and picked his way through the broken-down cars and trucks until he crossed the river; its thin band of water reflecting the orange glow all around.

"Hey, bud, where you goin'? You a medic?"

Wade cursed under his breath and reached behind to where his gun rested in its holster. He counted three of them, and his instincts—developed after three decades in the police—told him they were opportunist scum looking to make a quick buck out of the chaos.

"Out of my way," he said.

"Relax, dude, we're all friends here, ain't we boys?"

Wade put the leader in his late twenties. He was white and even in the reflected amber glow, Wade could see he was a user. Two other men stood behind him: one older, emaciated Black man, and a Latino who looked barely out of his teens.

"What do you want?"

"Well, I figure you're a paramedic and you might have something on you to help with the pain." He said it with a sarcastic smile as he pulled a handgun out of the waistband covered by his filthy Hawaiian shirt and held it in one hand, stroking it like a pet.

Wade could see the hunger in the man's expression. He must have known Wade would be unlikely to be carrying opioids, even if he was a paramedic, but was looking to steal whatever he could.

No time for this.

In one sudden movement, Wade brought the Colt Government out, swinging it through the air and catching the leader on the chin. He dropped like a stone, and Wade swept the gun back up, leveling it at the others as he grabbed the fallen leader's weapon.

They fell back, hands in the air.

"Throw the blades in the river," Wade said. "Now!"

The two accomplices glanced at each other, then down at their leader who was on the ground moaning, hand clenched around his jaw. Then they pitched the knives into the concrete channel and backed away.

Wade was watching this when the remaining thug, with a surprising burst of energy, leaped to his feet and lunged at him, the blade of a knife flashing in the moonlight.

Pure instinct took over as Wade leaned back and, as the wannabe mugger thrust out with his knife, aiming for Wade's gun hand, he dropped to the side and swung his elbow, hitting the ribs with a satisfying thunk. The attacker yelled, staggered and began tipping over the lip of the bridge as his feet slipped on the gritty sidewalk surface.

Wade could have grabbed the man's outstretched hand.

Maybe he should have done.

But he didn't.

He walked away as the thug fell toward the unforgiving river channel, his echoing cries ending in a sickening thud, followed by silence.

Wade ignored the other two as they looked down from the bridge. He had someone to save, and he couldn't help thinking that if he managed that, the scales of judgement would tip in his favor. A low-life mugger exchanged for an innocent woman's life. That's what he called justice.

***

He left them there, running across the road bridge and onto the boulevard. Lynch's place was somewhere along here, but most of the buildings he passed were commercial. A tower block rose dark against the orange sky, but his eye was caught by movement off to his left, the shattering of glass and excited shouts. Rioters. He couldn't see clearly, but he knew there was an electrical store there and he made out rectangular shapes being lifted through the broken windows. *Idiots—good luck turning those TVs on anytime soon.* His shoes crunched in the shattered glass of a pharmacy, and he glanced across to see shapes pushing over the display shelves and groveling in the mess.

He left them to it, though it clawed at his sense of what was right. As he jogged along, his lungs aching, his back hurting and his regret for his twenty-a-day habit nagging at him, he became more and more convinced that she would be alive. Something good had to come out of this nightmare, didn't it?

He glanced up. He could just make out faint stars and, off to one side, the half-moon. No sign of the aurora. *Grief, I wish I was twenty years younger*. He was exhausted in body and soul, and his burned back hurt like hell.

No sign of the emergency services. Had they given up? Or were they keeping their personnel inside for safety's sake as the police chief had said? It was a losing battle, in any case. For now, the streets belonged to the mob.

The stores and commercial properties gave way to apartments, and he knew he was close. Just as well, as his chest felt ready to explode and nausea rose from his stomach. *Keep going. She's depending on you.*

There it was. 429. Two blocks of apartments stacked two high faced each other at right angles to the road. It reminded him of a cheap motel. The sort of place a serial killer might hole up. Maybe on TV, but these apartments wouldn't have basements, and, for the first time, Wade began to wonder if he'd been played.

429 was on the first floor, on the end of the row. Most of the other apartments were dark, but candles flickered in one or two windows, and Wade decided to take care getting inside in case the neighbors assumed he was a looter and came out armed.

He unfolded his Swiss Army knife. It was the only thing his father had ever given him that he'd kept: a last-minute plea for forgiveness that Wade had accepted for his mother's sake. He subconsciously rubbed his shin, noticing the pain for the first time since he'd set off across the city. Another gift from his father.

Working the knife's blade down the door frame, he found the first lock and with practiced skill wiggled it backward. The doors in this apartment block were pretty basic, with sliding bolts that could only be fully locked from the inside. So, he focused on the second lock. *Man, it's hot.* He wiped his forehead with his arm and grunted as he worked on the door.

To his left, he could hear cries coming from the main street mixed in with the other sounds of a city in chaos. Not too close. Not a cause for concern right now. He just had to get inside and find her, then he could rest a while.

He sensed people in the other apartments watching him, but no one called or approached. Maybe it was his blue jacket which, in the flickering darkness, might have made him look like he was a police officer. More likely no one wanted trouble. How many of them had gone out today and were now feeling ill?

Come to think of it, how long outside would constitute deadly exposure? He'd been at his desk most of the day, but he'd gone out for lunch earlier and then driven across the city to try to get to the airport. Would he have been safe inside the car? Was he going to go the same way as Terry?

Focus!

With a final push, the lock gave in. Cheap garbage. Typical of landlords who cared more about being able to repossess their apartments than keeping the bad guys out. Or good guys in this case.

He pushed the door open, holding his Colt and flashlight together and sweeping the dark interior of the main living room. He got halfway inside, then stood still and listened. No movement.

The place gave every impression of being deserted, though it had a slightly unpleasant, all too human aroma.

He made his way to an open plan kitchen that smelled of bleach, then back into the living room and, at the opposite side to the kitchen, he found a small, offset corridor with three doors. The first led to a compact, meticulously clean bathroom. Then a tiny box-room dominated by an antique closet, and finally the main bedroom which had a window looking out front.

Wade checked under the bed, then went back through the house looking in every corner. There was no attic or basement and no sign of anyone. He cursed to himself. She wasn't here. All that effort as the city came apart around them and he'd believed that lying... He must have been renting somewhere else to keep his victims.

Elijah rubbed his temples, the nausea that had abated a little while he'd searched, returning with a vengeance. He couldn't face the journey back across the city just now, so he collapsed onto the sofa and leaned back, feeling his eyes starting to close.

Then his subconscious gave him a kick. There was something wrong about this place. Something didn't make sense. He sat there, replaying the tour he'd taken of the apartment. Living room, kitchen, bathroom, box room, bedroom.

The box room! It was too small! He jumped up and ran over to the corridor, pulling the door open. He went across to the closet and yanked the door.

It had clothes inside.

Women's clothes.

He pulled them out then, on a hunch, grabbed at the plywood back of the wardrobe. It gave way immediately, sliding to the left and revealing a hidden room. But this wasn't Narnia.

A woman lay on a narrow bed in her underwear, her hands and feet bound together with zip ties, and duct tape covering her mouth. The room stank of urine, and she looked at him with terror as he shined the flashlight at her.

"It's okay. I'm Detective Elijah Wade. Silas Lynch is in police custody. I'm here to get you out."

She shied away as he took the pen knife and cut the tape around her arms and legs, her eyes not moving from him for a moment. He paused, then showed her his badge. "You've been through a nightmare, but it's okay now." *Well*, he thought, *one of those two statements is true. Out of the frying pan?*

As soon as he'd untied her arms, she swung around on the bed, pulling herself back against the wall then ripped the duct tape from her mouth. "Why... why are you wearing a paramedic's jacket?"

"It's a long story. Things have gone crazy out there, but at least you're safe."

Still, she was looking beyond him as if frightened that this was some sort of trick.

Wade realized she needed space, so he stepped back, reversing out of the closet and she emerged warily.

"You are Rebecca, right?"

"Yeah. Becky. Why aren't the lights on?"

"That's another long story. The city's been hit by something."

"Can I go?"

"I'd rather you didn't. You've been through an ordeal, and I want to be sure you're okay."

"Me? What about you? You look like crap."

Wade rubbed his temples again. It felt as though his head was going to explode.

In that moment, she was past him.

"Come back!" he called, but she'd disappeared, escaping into the chaos outside.

He went to follow her, but tripped over his foot and collapsed, the dark swallowing him before he hit the floor.

4

Grace

"No sign of him," Walter Boone said, shaking his gray-haired head as he came through the door, and throwing his wide-brimmed hat onto its hook. Boomer, the German Shepherd, followed him inside and headed for the living room.

Grace shook her head. "That good for nothin'..." Then she jabbed a finger at her husband who was kicking off his boots. "You checked Sanchez's? And round the back of the grocery store?"

Wearily, Walter grunted acknowledgment. "Sure. I been all around. This ain't the first time I've gone lookin' for him, Gracie. I know what I'm doin'."

He shut the front door and made his way past his wife to the refrigerator, pulling out a bottle of Jester King and expertly removing the cap. "Rapture's comin'. You mark my words. I been tellin' you for thirty years. Foundation was right all along."

Grace Boone didn't like being wrong about anything, especially if it meant her husband was right. Brought up in a rural community, she'd met Walter at a church event and had, through him, become involved in The Foundation, a little-known offshoot of the Jehovah's Witnesses — their son, Lyle, called it a cult — and had moved to Walter's home state of Texas to prepare for the end times.

She'd gone along with it because she wanted to move away from the influence of her parents — now both long dead. But a marriage that had begun with little enough passion, was now as dry as the desert that encroach all around them. Frankly, she didn't care much one way or the other, but she wanted Lyle home to share it with them, and he'd spent the evening in the neighboring town drinking, fighting and, no doubt, fornicating. How two God-fearing people could produce such a low-life waster was beyond her. But she loved him, and she wished he was here.

She'd been watching the dancing lights as they'd become evident in the evening sky. Other folks had come out onto the road that ran past their cluster of gated compounds, but Grace remembered the lesson of Lot's wife and kept inside, for fear of directly witnessing the wrath of God.

Walter finished the bottle of beer and threw it in the recycling container before reaching for another.

"You take care; you know you can't take drink on your new medication," she said.

Wiping his forehead with the back of his arm, Walter opened the second bottle and took a drink. "Just this one — it's so darned hot."

Grace felt her husband's brow. "You got a fever comin'. You feel okay?"

Walter gave a dismissive gesture and headed out of the kitchen. "C'mon, inventory time."

"Are you kidding? Now?"

"Never been more serious in my life. Rapture's comin' and we need to be able to survive until our turn comes. If we wait 'till morning, it might be too late."

Grace sighed. She suspected that, despite his explanation, her husband was looking for something to keep himself occupied while they awaited news of their son. Or the end of the world arrived.

Walter led the way to the basement door and flicked on the light before heading down the wooden stairs. Though at first it might have appeared to be a perfectly ordinary basement, they'd extended it far beyond the foundations of the house, so it occupied the space under the back yard.

The original basement housed the items they might need in a hurry, including the forward armory and first aid station. Walter took a clipboard from a nail as he reached the bottom of the stairs and gestured at Grace to take her position.

She unlocked the grill door of the arms locker and waited for Walter to lick his pencil and begin the familiar roll call of weapons.

"Remington 870. Ruger 10/22. Colt AR-15."

Grace read them all out as Walter ticked them off.

"Savage 24."

She heard him sigh. Sure, it was her peccadillo. A rifle that could shoot one .22 round and one .410 shell seemed pointless to her husband, but as far as she was concerned, the smaller round would deal with a coyote or snake and the bigger one would handle any human. She was a good shot, and one round would do it. Its lightness and basic simplicity were the main reasons she liked it. And it had just enough killing power to keep her safe without blowing her target apart.

She reached the hand-gun rack. Walter had his Glock 19 on his belt, so these were backups. "Ruger Single-Ten, Ruger Single-Six." The latter was hers — she hadn't wanted a revolver, but Walter had insisted.

She then listed the ammunition which was, of course, exactly the same as last time. Or was it?

"Hold on. You counted those .22 boxes right, Gracie? I got four hundred rounds here, that's eight boxes."

Grace double checked. "Darn it. I only count six."

"That son of a bitch!"

"Lyle!" Grace said, spitting his name like a curse.

Walter kicked out at the bottom stair, then grunted in pain.

"I knew he owed money to some no-good dealer in Twisted Pine. Guess he figured he could pay in ammunition."

"But he knew we'd find out!"

Grace shrugged. "He ain't been thinkin' straight lately. Maybe he thought he could replace the rounds before we took another stock check; we're not due for three weeks."

"What did we do wrong? Sure feels like some kind of punishment to be saddled with the likes of him. We brought him up to be a good Christian boy, ready to join the Foundation, and what did we get? He's practically a atheist!"

Grace patted her husband on the arm. "Come on, let's get the inventory done. See if he's taken anything else from his own flesh and blood."

Picking up the clipboard, Walter sighed and made a note of the missing ammunition. "He'd better hope I don't never find him or he's gonna wish he was dead."

Grace followed him into the dry store area. Here, they had a circulation system in which air was drawn into the basement through a duct leading to the outside. A wind turbine at the top of the shaft produced a slight vacuum and a second, smaller shaft equalized the pressure, bringing dry desert air inside.

She ran her finger down the metal racks reading out the sacks, boxes and cans. They had pasta — spaghetti, penne and macaroni — and a huge box of individually sealed packs of ramen. Two types of rice, oats, flour and corn meal. Sugar, salt, corn starch and powdered milk occupied the next shelves, followed by a smaller section that held baking and cooking supplies: including yeast, baking powder and salt.

The canned food section was part of the extended basement, and they moved quickly through the fruits, vegetables, meats and beans before reaching the rows of preserves that she'd made herself. She was particularly proud of the chutneys — made using a basic recipe handed down from her British great grandmother.

They were about to tackle the refrigerator and freezer when Walter sighed and leaned against the wall. "Let's take a break, Gracie. I sure feel beat."

She checked his temperature again. "You're burnin' up! And what's that on your neck? Looks like a hickey."

She pulled down his collar to reveal a livid red sore. "What in the name of heaven is this?" Then her face froze. "You been out under the dancin' angels?"

"Is that what you're callin' them? Well, I didn't have a whole lot of choice, did I? But I was in the truck most of the time. They sure looked pretty, though. Lots of people was out on the roads, all starin' up at the sky. Poor fools don't know what's comin'.'"

She took his arm and guided him back toward the stairs. "Well, you need to get to bed. Whatever's ailing you ain't gonna get no better until you have some rest."

He struggled up the steps, even with her help, and she had a devil of a job to get him to his bedroom overlooking the back of the house. They hadn't shared a bed for ten years, but she brought in the fold up bed they kept for their occasional visitors and set it up on the bedroom floor. This had been the bed their niece, Abby, had used when she'd come to stay. Before her father had put a stop to it. She wondered where the girl might be now, and prayed that at least some of what she'd taught her had sunk in.

She was more worried by the fact that Walter didn't protest about her bed being in his room than she was about his fever, or the sore. But then, when she helped him off with his shirt, she saw that his torso was covered in blotches, some of them bruise-like, others looking like ulcers.

"My God, Walt. Did you get into a fight you didn't tell me about? Lyle didn't do this, did he?"

Walter grunted as he ran his hand over his forehead. "What are you talkin' about? No, I told you, I didn't see Lyle. But sweet Lord, I feel bad. Real bad."

She left him there, watched over by the anxious Boomer, heading downstairs to fetch a wet cloth and some water. She took some Advil from the drugs chest and returned to find him half-asleep and moaning quietly.

"Here, take a couple of these."

He didn't argue, but just settled back with a grunt of pain once he'd taken his pills. Within minutes he'd fallen into a restless slumber, and she was left to watch him. Through the window, she could see the angels dancing in the sky.

She got up and pulled the drapes closed. It couldn't do any good for mortal eyes to witness the war in the heavens. This was the beginning, she was certain. But she wanted to face it with Walter. She'd thought she hated him, but now he was so sick, she wasn't so certain. She sure didn't want him to die. Maybe his body would heal, and they could go looking for Lyle once the angels had gone back to Heaven.

#

Day 2

The following morning, it seemed to her that Walter was a little better. His temperature had dropped, and he'd taken the oatmeal she'd offered him gratefully.

She'd had a fitful night herself, waking up time and again to check on him and the display outside. The lights had finally faded a few hours after Walter had gone to bed and, to her shame, she'd felt relieved when it had happened. She should welcome the end of days, but she couldn't help but be afraid of Heaven's wrath.

Walter got himself dressed, insisting on showering alone and seeming almost normal when he joined her in the kitchen.

"Reckon we'd better do a perimeter walk before we check on the neighbors."

"Are you sure you're up to it?"

He rolled his eyes. "Stop fussing, woman. I don't know what it was, but I feel better today. We've got things to do, so let's get to it."

"At least let me check your sores."

"I said stop fussin'!"

Their ranch was on a plot of around an acre, but they'd erected a fence that extended around a fourth of that, and this was their defensive perimeter.

"You stay while I head up to the lookout," she said, trying not to react to the obvious relief on his face at not having to tackle the ladder that led onto the roof.

It was hard enough for her. She'd sailed past sixty years in this life a while ago now, and she'd never been the most athletic woman. So, she was blowing by the time she emerged through the trapdoor into the morning son, grunting as she got onto her knees and hauled herself upright, grabbing onto the rail.

It was chilly up here, the wind rippling her pants as she kept a tight hold and looked down. Their house was set a hundred feet back from an asphalt road that connected them with the main highways of the state. Theirs was the first for half a mile or so, but a dozen other houses lined up along their side of the road, and opposite, each separated by a strip of land from the next one. The community extended for a full mile along the strip, as it was known locally, and it *was* a community, despite the distance between each house.

Walter had been instrumental in laying a surplus military telephone cable along the road. He and the neighbors had dug a trench and every neighbor who'd wanted one had bought a compatible military phone that was powered by batteries. It was primitive, and generally only used on special occasions — and only then for fun — but had come into its own when the power had gone out for a week a couple of years back.

Once they'd walked the perimeter, she'd call up the nearest neighbors and make sure they were okay. As okay as you could be given the circumstances. None of them belonged to The Foundation, but all were God fearing

Christians. She hoped they'd accompany her in the Rapture, even the Johnsons, who were Catholics and were about to find out that all they'd believed was wrong.

She swung away from the road, briefly glancing at the nearest houses, cursing at herself for not putting her glasses on, and then looked out. The fence formed a rectangle centered on their land that fronted the road, with a central gate. To the back, it encompassed the little market garden she was so proud of, fed by water drawn up from the well. They had shooting positions in the four corners of the house, giving them a clear line of sight to all parts of the enclosed area, unless any attackers got very close and disappeared under the eaves.

From where she stood, the turbine was hidden behind the house, but she could hear it gently turning in the wind, generating the power that fed the underground lithium battery. That, and the roof's solar panels that glinted black in the morning sun, provided more than enough power to run the house, including the freezer and refrigerator in the basement, and the surveillance cameras. They'd disconnected from the main power grid after the recent outage and had been self-sufficient ever since.

She heard Walter's voice calling from below. He always griped that she spent too long up here, but it was so nice. It gave her a sense of security and pride. Other folks could call them crazy, but, as far as she was concerned, that was just another word for prepared.

Grace climbed down the ladder into what had once been their attic but was now a storage area and secondary armory.

When she made it to the first floor, Walter was leaning against the wall. He looked drawn and exhausted, and Grace could see the sore extending up his neck. "Are you sure you're okay? Why don't I check the perimeter myself? I can call the neighbors when I get back."

He shook his head. "I'll come with you. Did you eyeball the perimeter from the roof?"

"Sure I did."

"Then we can skip that."

"What? Seriously?"

He gestured through the living room door to the TV. "TV's not working. We got power, but it won't turn on."

"What about the one in the basement?"

"I ain't got the energy to go down there. But Brandon'll know what's going on. Maybe an EMP."

Grace gripped his arm in surprise but released her grip as he flinched in pain. "I'm sorry, Walt. But if it's an EMP, it ain't the Rapture."

"You think the good Lord can't wipe out the electronics? C'mon, let's go find Brandon, then I'll take some more Advil. Unless we got somethin' stronger?"

The medical supplies were Grace's responsibility and, though Walter had very strong views about narcotics, she'd included some morphine in her inventory, figuring that if either of them broke a leg they'd need more than ibuprofen to see them through it.

The fact that he didn't complain when she suggested it told her all she needed to know about the pain he was in.

When they finally emerged from the house, Walter was carrying his shotgun openly, while Grace had her Ruger in a concealed holster under her linen jacket. Boomer trotted warily beside them, head darting from side to side.

Walter opened the gate and checked along the road for any sign of movement. Nothing. It was a quiet backroad, but there was usually something moving. But then, a strong enough EMP would knock out most modern vehicles.

"It's so quiet," she said.

Walter put his hand up. "It would be if you'd put a lid on it, woman!"

She was going to protest — she didn't take that kind of attitude from anyone, even her husband. But he merely pointed along the road.

A figure, limping along, arm outstretched, as if pleading for help.

"Who the hell is that?" Walter asked.

She screwed up her eyes, but the figure was too far away. "My Lord, have the tombs opened? Walter? Have the dead come to life?"

5

Hannah

Hannah knew something was wrong as soon as she came around, woken up by an excited babble from somewhere above her bedroom. Generally, the astronomers and staff of the Mercury Observatory went about their business quietly, but, right now, she needed sleep and she wasn't getting it. Glancing at the old-fashioned mechanical clock on her bed stand, she cursed: working the day shift sucked.

"Give me a break." She'd been in bed for no more than a couple of hours and it would barely be dark outside. Why the excitement? It sounded like a party. But these were astronomers, so she immediately struck that possibility out. Maybe it was to do with the flare.

She was equal parts angry at being woken, and curious, so there was no point in trying to go back to sleep. She got up and swung her legs over the side of her bed, flicking her bedside lamp on and illuminating her spartan room — one of a block made of shipping containers buried beneath the observatory proper.

Pulling on a pair of loose pants and her official observatory fleece, she slipped on her clogs and headed into the dark corridor outside before climbing the steel stairs to the observatory's ground floor.

"Cool, you're awake!"

Hannah caught sight of her friend as she ran in from the main entrance. "Hey, Priti. What's going on? Sounds like everyone's been on the shandy again."

"I was just about to come down and wake you up," Priti Hussain said. "You can't miss this."

Priti grabbed Hannah's hand and dragged her toward the entrance as it swung open to reveal a young man who staggered inside, his hand across his forehead.

"Lester! You look like—" Hannah began, but Priti was pulling her past the forlorn figure and out under the night sky.

It looked like just about everyone was out here, even Director LaRoche, and they were all looking up.

"Oh my God," Hannah gasped as she gazed upward. The normal perfect black of the sky above Mauna Kea, Hawaii with its gently shining ribbon of milky cream had been completely overwhelmed by a shimmering kaleidoscope of color. She'd seen the aurora borealis on a trip to Lapland, but this made that look like the moment in *The Wizard of Oz* when the picture goes from monochrome to color. "Spectacular," she gasped.

Her mouth wide with amazement, she did an inventory and found every hue imaginable, though blues and purples outnumbered reds and oranges. And there was a strange sound, like an ethereal song, that vied with the wind.

"Isn't it incredible?" Priti said, in a breathless whisper. "Once in a lifetime."

"What's the theory?" Hannah asked. Her friend's words had snapped her out of the trance and her scientific mind was now whirring.

Keeping her eyes cast upward, Priti gestured at the crowd. "Bixby says it's a cloud of interstellar gas."

"Who's taking measurements?"

"What? Oh, I don't know. It's all being recorded. We can check later. Let's just look for once. With our own eyes."

Hannah looked at her friend. Priti by name and pretty by nature, she was a formidable astrophysicist. She'd met her when Priti had come from Pakistan to study at Oxford. This wasn't like her. It was as if she'd been enchanted. "I'm going to take a look."

Priti sagged. "Seriously? You English are all the same. All work and no play."

"You obviously haven't met many Brits," she responded. "But I'm going to check anyway. Be back soon." Stalking off, Hannah left her friend there staring up at the wonder above. If Heaven existed — and Hannah had seen no evidence to suggest it did — she guessed its skies would look like this.

Lester Schmidt was slumped on a plastic chair in the entranceway. "What's up, Les? Have you come down with something?"

The young man lifted his head as she crouched beside him. "I'm burning up. Feels like COVID again."

"Can't be, we're all vaccinated, and no one's been in or out for over a week." One of the advantages of working at the remotest observatory of a group set atop a volcano on an island in the middle of the Pacific was that infectious diseases didn't have much chance to get a foothold. But Hannah instinctively backed away on her heels, resisting the temptation to feel the man's forehead. "Do you want me to get you into bed?"

"Thought you'd never ask," he responded with a cheeky smile.

Hannah blushed and got to her feet. "You can't be feeling too bad. Look, I'm going to the control room, but if you're still here when I get back, I'll give you a hand."

She heard him grunt with amusement again as she marched away but didn't turn back. She was thirty-four, carrying a little extra around her tummy and, in her opinion at least, only vaguely attractive when seen in certain lights and from particular angles. But in a male dominated profession at a remote location, she knew that some of the more testosterone-infused members of the team regarded her as a suitable port in the storm of celibacy.

He was probably watching her as she ran up the stairs. Feeling herself getting hotter, she cursed herself for wearing sloppy pants that did nothing to keep her backside under any kind of order. Gravity was inexorable, as was her father's Ghanaian ancestry.

With relief, she pulled at the glass door to the control room and glanced around in case her embarrassment was too obvious. The lights were customarily low in here, but there was no one to see her anyway. They were all down below taking in this unique event.

As she crossed to the instrument panel, she wondered if she was missing out. After all, it was one thing to watch a recording of the aurora, quite another to see it with your own eyes. But something was bugging her. It was probably nothing, but science was about having a cool, rational head and not losing yourself in the moment. She sighed. Her nickname at school had been Mrs. Robot, and she'd always resisted getting carried away emotionally, feeling a little jealous of those who could let themselves entirely go, experiencing life in its full glory while she analyzed all the joy out of it.

"Good God," she said, jerking herself out of her malaise. The Field Emission Array recorded the strength of the electromagnetic radiation that made it through the atmosphere. This meant everything from ultraviolet to radio waves. And the readings were off the chart, especially at the shorter end of the spectrum. The people gazing up at the aurora were going to suffer from a hell of a case of sunburn if they didn't put on some factor fifty.

She was about to go find Director LaRoche and warn him that everyone should protect themselves when a thought struck her, so she crossed over to one of the computers and dialed up the feed from XRSAT. It detected short wavelengths: gamma radiation and x-rays that were usually absorbed by the Earth's atmosphere and, therefore, undetectable from the ground, even as high up as they were here.

Her mouth dropped open as the raw data came in. The values were so high, she had to scroll back until she found normal numbers so she could be sure she understood the scale they were using. Then, quite abruptly, they stopped. The satellite's signal had vanished. Feeling herself going numb, she sent all the data to the printer and then, as the most recent measurements before the blackout appeared, she snatched up the paper and ran out of the control room.

She barely noticed Lester Schmidt as he sat, slumped in a corner, his face white and his eyes closed. She tore past him, pulled open the front door and sought Director LaRoche. The crowd had thinned a little, even though the lightshow was becoming, if anything, even more spectacular. There was something odd about the way people were moving. She saw Priti leaning against a wall, a glass of wine in her hand, staring into nothing as if she were lost in thought. And there was an ethereal sound of singing in the air.

"Director LaRoche!!" Hannah called. The director — a large man in his early sixties — turned around slowly.

"What is it, doctor?"

She handed him the data summary sheet, then watched as he moved his glasses down his nose before, finally, taking them off entirely and squinting at the figures inches from his face.

"*Ce n'est pas possible!* There must be some mistake."

Hanna jabbed a finger at the printout. "It's the raw data, I haven't touched anything. I don't know where the x-rays are coming from, but they're causing the aurora, and we're standing here, taking a hell of a dose."

He shook his head, but his eyes remained wide. "It cannot be. The Earth's atmosphere absorbs wavelengths as short as these."

"We've never seen readings like this," Hannah insisted. "Without a Geiger counter, we have no way of knowing whether they're reaching ground level, but what if they are?"

Then she remembered Lester Schmidt, and the odd way people were moving. "Director, we've got to get inside! See if we can fix up one of the ultraviolet rigs to give us a rough reading. People are getting sick already!"

There was a lifelessness to the man's face as he looked at her with unfocused eyes.

She didn't have time to wait for him to make a decision.

"Everybody inside!" she bellowed, her voice echoing around the three-sided courtyard.

The low murmur that had been all that was left of the party spirit by the time she'd returned from the control room disappeared, and a dozen faces turned in her direction.

She gestured desperately toward the entrance. "The aurora is associated with high energy radiation! We've got to get under cover!"

Priti was the first to react. She looked across at Hannah, gave a weak nod and began staggering toward shelter.

"Director, come on!" Hannah hauled on the man's thick arm as an administrator took his other one. She imagined she could feel the radiation heating her brain as they made their painfully slow way across the courtyard. At least, she hoped it was her imagination.

Finally, they got inside.

"He's dead!"

Someone was kneeling beside the body of Lester Schmidt.

Hannah left the director to the care of others and looked down on the young man she'd so recently been silently accusing of lecherous intent. His white face was punctuated by red sores that, as she watched, seem to be spreading even after life had so obviously departed. His bloodshot eyes stared sightlessly up at the ceiling and, beyond it, the roiling heavens.

"He was the one who spotted the aurora first," the kneeling man said. She recognized him as a cosmologist called Claude Remy from a university in Paris, France. He cursed under his breath. "So stupid! Are we not scientists? To fall under the spell of something so beautiful without making measurements. We leave it to machines, and this is the result."

Hannah wiped a tear from her cheek as he got up and withdrew himself from the crowd of people gathered around the body. He took her arm and pulled her close.

"Many of us are going to get sick very soon, Doctor Redman."

She nodded, surprised that he even knew her name. She couldn't think of a single conversation they'd had.

"You were not so exposed, I think?"

"I was in bed. Then I saw the aurora and ..."

"You did what others should have — you checked the instruments. You are the best of us, Hannah. But now, you must check the quarters downstairs for anyone else who was sheltered — *merde* we have been fools. I will call for help."

Call for help. Her parents! Her fiancé! She had to warn them. She pulled out her cell, found the contact marked *Oni* and dialed her mother. It would be routed to England via the observatory cluster's satellite link and cost her a fortune, but she didn't care.

"I'm sorry," a mechanical voice said, "your call cannot be connected. Please try again later or contact support using reason '#404 Uplink Unavailable'".

Of course! If the XRSAT readings were accurate, they would be frying orbital communications — perhaps permanently destroying the satellites the world had come to rely on. Just in case, she tried again and got the same message. Cursing, she decided she would have to deal with the crisis at hand before worrying about how to get in touch with them.

She put her cell back in her pocket and went to go but bumped into Priti who was hugging a tall scientist.

"How are you?" Hannah asked, feeling as though she was interrupting a private moment.

Priti shook her head silently. Then whispered, "We're going to die." The man she was hugging heaved, and Hannah thought he was crying, but then a stream of bloody vomit erupted from him, hitting the wall behind Priti. She pushed him away, and he fell to the floor, his head landing with a thud.

"Oh my God!" she sobbed, kneeling beside the stricken figure and pulling him onto his back.

Hannah looked over her shoulder. She knew the man by sight, but not his name as he'd only recently arrived. And now, she never would know him. If he wasn't dead by now, he would be soon enough.

She put her hands on her friend's shoulder. "I'm sorry. But we've got to help those we can still save. We don't have time to grieve yet."

"It's too late. We've all been exposed. All except you."

"Look, we don't know what the lethal dosage is," Hannah said. "Professor Remy is calling for help, so we only have to hold on for a while. I'm going to see if anyone slept through this madness."

She wasn't sure if Priti had heard her, but there was no time to waste, so she left her there and headed back down the metal staircase to the sleeping quarters.

There were ten bedrooms down here; just shipping containers with minimal furniture. She'd seen more comfortable prison cells. But if she was right and radiation had somehow made its way through the atmosphere, then these metal boxes might act as Faraday cages, protecting those sleeping within. And the fact that they had the observatory above them and were dug into the ground meant they were the safest place to be.

The first three rooms contained sick partygoers, each lying on their beds. She knew them all — the shipping containers were for the junior staff, and they'd formed something of a community — but she got little response other than moaning and sobs.

She crossed her fingers when the opened the fourth door. This was Shane Walsh's room, and he was on the same rotation as she was. He didn't know him that well, but he seemed like a typical Aussie, inhabiting the mantle of Crocodile Dundee while claiming Paul Hogan was just a stereotype. But she'd take any able-bodied help right now. Had he also been woken by the noise and gone outside?

It was dark inside, the light coming in from the corridor revealing a bed which looked like an island in a sea of discarded clothes. A body lay on its side on the mattress, facing away from her, the bed clothes gathered around its shoulders.

"Shane?" she said, half whispering out of habit.

No movement, no sound, except for the moaning coming from the rooms on either side and the metallic thunk of footsteps above them.

She held her breath and picked her way to where he lay. She shook his shoulder. "Shane?"

Instantly, he was all arms and legs, pulling himself up and looking around. "Jesus! What the hell?" Earplugs landed on the pillow as he brought his eyes into focus and recognized her. "Hannah?"

"Yeah, it's me."

"What's going on? Fire drill?"

"No drill, Shane. We were talking about extinction events the other day. Remember?"

He nodded, puzzled. "Sure. Ordovician, Permian, Cretaceous. The last one took out the dinosaurs. Hold on, we're going to be hit by an asteroid?"

"No. This could be worse. Much worse."

6

Hannah

Hannah and Shane were climbing the stairs when the lights died. From above and below, they heard cries of dismay, but together they felt their way to the ground floor of the observatory.

She'd spent hundreds of hours up here at night, so she knew it intimately. Shaped like a cylinder, offices and laboratories clustered around a central pillar with stainless steel stairways linking the three above-ground floors. But though she'd been up here at night, there had always been low level red lights to guide her way, and the blinking of computer screens and instrument panels that were now entirely dead, as were some of the shapes lying silently in a darkness punctuated by moans of pain and despair.

"The backup generator's along here," Shane said, grabbing her by the hand and leading her to one side of the cylinder. He'd taken her summary of what had happened in typically phlegmatic fashion, though she suspected he was simply not processing it for now. She wished she had a switch like that — her mind was whirring around whether it was constructive or not.

She put her other arm out and looked through the corners of her eyes to try to discern anything familiar in the reflected light coming in from outside. They made it to the far side and, once her eyes had adjusted, she could make out faint, rippling colors playing across the white wall. So, the aurora was still alive. She wondered how many of the people who'd looked up at it could say the same.

"Have you got your smartphone?" Shane asked.

Hannah cursed at herself. *Get a grip on yourself!* She'd had it in her pocket along. Cells were of limited use up here, but hers had a flashlight.

She didn't dare look behind to where she knew there must be bodies lying, so she shone it into the small room containing the generator.

"It's supposed to come on automatically if the main power goes," he said, kneeling at the small control panel as Hannah held the phone pointed at the readout.

"The RCD's gone," she said, spotting the thick switch in the off position.

Shane nodded and pushed the rocker up. Instantly, the generator chugged into life and, moments later, the emergency lighting activated.

"We'd better go find LaRoche," Hannah said. "Or Remy — maybe he was able to get through to the emergency services."

Shane made a non-committal noise. "I reckon they may be pretty busy. Unless we're only seeing it because we're at high altitude."

She led him out of the generator room and toward the central stairs. Scattered around the edge of the cylindrical room, she could see shapes, some covered up, others not. A few moved fitfully and she kneeled beside one that she recognized.

"Priti." Her friend was ruined. Gone was the vivacious young scientist, replaced by a shell of herself, as if she'd aged a hundred years in a couple of hours. Her hair had turned white, and her brown skin was falling off in pieces that lay around her head like fallen leaves.

She opened her eyes, and they were white and sightless. "Please." She looked like someone who'd been put in a microwave oven.

"I'm so sorry," Hannah said, tears falling as she gazed at this husk of her friend. "I don't know what I can do."

Shane appeared beside her and handed over a med kit. "Oh my God. Priti."

She said one word. "Pain."

Hannah opened the med kit. "This is just first aid. Sit with her, will you? I'm going to find the strong stuff."

She left Shane there, his eyes moving from the ruin of their friend to the skies he could see through the double thickness glass that run around the top of the cylinder. Were they receiving a heavy dose even inside? So far, aside from a headache and a slight fever, Hannah hadn't felt anything unusual, so she was pretty sure the main exposure came from being outside, but without any means of measuring it, she couldn't be sure how big a dose she'd taken.

She climbed to the second floor and the small medical bay that served them all. The place was a mess, but whoever had been in here had focused on pills, and she was looking for something intravenous. She found what she needed, scooped up a pack of iodine tablets that had been half hidden under the examination table, and went back downstairs.

Hannah Redman had wanted to be a medical doctor but had switched track a year into her course when she realized how unsuited she was to the profession. She'd volunteered at a local animal rescue and had seen what happened to very sick animals who had no chance of survival. They did the difficult, but kind thing.

She returned to find Priti weeping weakly.

"I don't know what to do," Shane said, his face wet. "She cries out when I touch her. Jeez, Hannah, what do we do?"

Hannah took the vial of morphine and inserted the hypodermic syringe.

"What are you doing?" Shane asked, though he knew the answer well enough.

Looking down at Priti, she said, "Do you want to go to sleep, Priti? You'll never be in pain again."

Priti let out a huge sob of relief, then nodded and, with a great effort, managed to lift her hand, the only visible part of her that wasn't covered in sores. Shane wrapped both hands around it, then looked at Hannah through his tears.

Hannah withdrew the syringe and kneeled beside her friend. Priti flinched as the red flesh of her arm was exposed, but Hannah held her tight with one hand while she found the vein on the inside of her elbow and carefully but without hesitating, plunged it in and emptied the syringe.

It took only moments for Priti to go still, and minutes for her to stop breathing.

And it was then, once she'd done what had to be done, that Hannah Redman sat on the polished floor and wept.

#

"Doctor Redman."

She wiped her eyes and looked up to see the tall figure of Claude Remy standing over her. Shane helped her get to her feet and she looked into the cosmologist's blotchy face. She guessed he hadn't been exposed for as long as poor Priti, but it would likely be enough to kill him. She'd seen *Chernobyl*, though this was happening much faster.

"I could not raise anyone to come to our aid, and I fear it is too late for most of us. Doctor Walsh, did you stay below?"

"Yeah," Shane said.

"Then you must look after Doctor Redman."

"I'm okay," Hannah said, feeling her blood turn to ice.

Remy shook his head. "*Non*. Everyone who was outside for more than a short while has been exposed to a high dose. You, perhaps, the least. But you may become ill and so I ask Doctor Walsh to care for you. I have also secured a supply of iodine tablets for you both. I do not know if they will help, but I hope so."

Shane put his arm around Hannah. "And Director LaRoche?"

"Dead. I fear billions more will follow him, but we have no way of knowing. Communications are down, even now that the power has been restored, and of course so is the internet. Perhaps it will return, but for now we are isolated. Much of our equipment has been rendered useless by the electromagnetic wave, but I have got the ultraviolet detector working. It seems likely that the radiation is across the spectrum, so when the U.V. shows high, we can assume high levels at short wavelengths also. Here."

He handed a small device to Shane. "This is working at present, but I suggest you shield it."

"Have you tried contacting the other observatories?"

Remy nodded sadly. "It was possible for a short time, but they are in the same situation as us. Now, I must ask you to aid where you can." He swayed and put his hand to his head, his breath coming in short pants as if he were in sudden pain.

"Here, let me help you," Shane said.

"Thank you. If you take me to my quarters ... then you can leave me. My end is coming, and I wish to meet it on my own terms, not like poor Doctor Hussain. Good luck."

Hannah watched as Shane put his arm under Remy's shoulders and took the professor's weight, guiding him toward the quarters of the senior staff on the second floor.

She found a blanket and laid it over Priti's body, the tears coming again as she covered her friend's head. She'd been so beautiful. Hannah detected the edges of shock closing in on her but fought to keep the blackness away. She was needed.

She couldn't sense any fever when ran her fingers over her forehead, but she definitely had a migraine brewing, and she felt sick to her stomach. That might have been due to the shock and disgust of what had happened in no more than a couple of hours, or it might have been the first signs of radiation poisoning. She took one of the iodine pills, washing it down with water from her bottle.

Good grief, if she was right and the aurora was caused by broad spectrum radiation at levels like a nuclear explosion, then that could sterilize the planet — of animal life at least.

Shane had given her the ultraviolet monitor and she glanced at the line graph display. The levels had dropped precipitously over the past half an hour, so she risked a look outside and found that the aurora had disappeared. Hope rose in her heart. If whatever had caused the aurora had now faded, then only part of the Earth's surface might have been affected. This side of the planet could have been irradiated, but the other side might have escaped. It would be a catastrophe, for sure, but planet Earth and humanity would survive. If the aurora had lasted twenty-four hours, then the world would have been roasted like a pig on a spit with no part of it escaping.

"What are you doing out here?" Shane called as she stood in the darkness outside.

"The levels have dropped," she said, as if that were explanation enough. Coming back inside, she said, "How's Remy?"

Shane shook his head. "Probably dead by now. He's a type one diabetic, and he has enough insulin to kill himself ten times over. Not a bad way to go, I reckon. How are you feeling?"

"I'm okay. A bit tired and nauseous, and I've got a humdinger of a headache coming, but I don't think I caught much of a dose."

"I'm glad."

She put her hand on his shoulder as if using him for support. "What do we do now?"

"I guess we help our colleagues and friends as best we can."

"All we have is painkillers and insulin."

He took her hand and looked into her eyes. His square face and large jaw meant he wasn't a handsome man, but she felt a connection between the two of them that brought a little comfort. "If that's all we've got, then that's what we'll use. But it isn't about drugs, it's about caring. And let's hope that at least one or two of them can survive this."

"Let's hope," she said.

#

Shane volunteered to go back down to the sleeping quarters and check on those who'd taken to their beds. Hannah had tried to insist she go, but in truth she was feeling progressively worse and wasn't sure how much help she would be to the sick down there. So she struggled up two flights of stairs to the control center at the top of the observatory, where she'd first seen the scale of the disaster in figures.

Someone was sitting in a swivel chair, head resting on swollen hands. It was Kuchinsky, a Russian physicist here on an exchange program. She thought he must be dead, but as she made her way to a terminal on the other side of the small room, he stirred.

"*Kto ty*?"

"I'm sorry, I don't speak Russian," she said, crossing the room reluctantly and pulling up a chair.

"Of course. My mind is not ... working."

"Is there anything I can get you?"

He grunted. "*Grach.*" Then, as he saw she didn't understand, he pointed a finger at his head and mimed pulling the trigger.

She didn't know how to respond, so she tried to change the subject. "Have you tried to contact anyone?"

"No one to contact, I think. *Vymiraniye.* Extinction."

She wasn't ready to face that thought, though she knew that whatever had happened was certainly catastrophic. "Do you have a theory?"

"Not enough data. I think, maybe, interstellar debris. Solar system passes through it. Sun makes it go boom, like Molotov cocktail. Maybe supernova remnant. Does not matter."

She rubbed her chin, trying to clear the fog in her mind so she could consider his hypothesis, and then felt his hand on her arm.

"Please. Help me. Get my pistol. I will do rest. So … so much pain."

She looked at his tortured face. What could she say? She'd helped dear Priti on her way, God forgive her, didn't this man deserve the same mercy? It wasn't as if she was going to pull the trigger herself.

"Where is it?"

"In my quarters." He fumbled in his pocket and handed over a key. "Please be quick."

She left him there, lying face down on the desk, twitching and, from time to time, letting out a low moan.

Visiting scientists were put up in the senior staff block — a series of half a dozen pods built into the walls of the observatory with views looking out over the volcanic landscape or, at least, so she'd been told. She'd never been invited inside one of them.

She climbed the stairs to the top level and found Kuchinsky's room, turning the key to unlock it. It was remarkably tidy inside — the sleeping quarters under the observatory ranged from scruffy to, as in Shane's case, filthy. The bed had been made, and on the nightstand beside it, she saw a photo of a smiling woman holding a young child at her hip.

She checked in the drawer to find a Cyrillic Bible and, at the back, a handgun. It looked to her to be pretty old but well maintained, and she wondered what Kuchinsky's background was. Perhaps it had belonged to his father. Well, she would never know now.

Hannah turned to go, but she couldn't take her eyes off the photo of the smiling woman. His wife, presumably. She was on the other side of the world so, perhaps, she'd escaped the lights. Hannah hoped so. She felt as though she would have liked this woman.

She went over to the wide window that looked out into the darkness of Mauna Kea's summit. She turned off the lights and waited for her eyes to adjust, hoping to catch at least some signs of life out there.

Then, she looked up and realized that clouds had formed above them because, quite abruptly, they parted and, beyond them, she saw a rainbow aurora pulsing in the sky.

She ran out of the room, calling out to Shane, but, as she reached the top of the downward stairs, the storm in her mind that had been threatening for the past couple of hours finally broke. The rainbow swum across her vision as she twisted around, her legs went out from under her, and she fell into space.

7

Abby & Rae

Day 1: California

Abby watched her half-sister open the gate, then drove the car inside and parked it in front of the cabin. She'd been here every Christmas for the past twenty years, but for the last decade, she'd arrived on her own ahead of the rest of the family so she could enjoy having the place to herself for a few days.

Not this year, though. This year, her dad had insisted she make a detour to fetch Rae and nothing she said could dissuade him. She must have sounded like a spoiled brat as she whined about this being the only chance she had to be alone, but it cut no ice.

Behind her, she could hear Rae running from the gate. "Slow down!" she called, waving a warning at the girl. The last thing she needed was to have to deal with another attack.

Rae, who was clearly under instructions to be on her best behavior, walked the rest of the way. "I love it here," she said, arriving to stand beside Abby.

"Me too."

"Don't say it like that."

"Like what?" She looked down at her sister who, at fifteen was far too sharp for her liking.

"'*Me* too?' You didn't want to pick me up."

There was no point denying it. "No, I didn't. But you're here now."

"I'll be as quiet as a mouse."

"Sure you will."

"There it is again!"

Abby walked up the wooden steps and pulled the key out of her pocket. She breathed in the smell of the place — cedar and wood preservative, in the main — and opened the front door.

Good, Mrs. Liu had been in and given the place a good clean as she did every year. Despite that, the cabin had the feel of a place that hadn't been lived in, but she knew that would evaporate as soon as her father arrived. And his wife.

She put that thought to the back of her mind and flicked on the light switch, taking in the familiar scene. The cabin was all on one level, and consisted of a large, open living room with a brick-built hearth and a kitchen to one side. A door in the left wall led to the master bedroom, and straight ahead, beyond the fireplace, was the door to two more rooms where she and Rae slept.

"It feels good to be back, doesn't it?" Rae said, skipping past Abby and flinging her backpack on the couch.

"It does." And she meant it. She'd wanted to be alone here, but the place made her happy, even in her half-sister's presence. *Don't forget not to call her that. Dad hates it because Monika wants to pretend we're all one happy family.* No, she was to call Rae sister. After fifteen years, she'd probably earned that right, but Abby couldn't help but resent the impact that woman had had on her family. And her father, of course.

"I'm going to make my bed," Rae said, heading through to the bedrooms.

For a moment at least, Abby *was* alone.

It was a far cry from her life in Seattle, but then that was the point. They'd first come to Redwood Grove, CA as a family when she was a toddler, spending the summer holidays here and returning for a couple of weeks over Christmas. Her father was a media executive working out of LA, and so while she was a child, they'd make the trek to the cabin as a family.

They'd carried on with the tradition even after he'd met Monika Wang, model and reality TV star, and divorced his wife and Abby's mother. As she'd matured, Abby had worked out that the story wasn't as simple as it seemed on the surface — or as her mom painted it — but the betrayal at the heart of it had made it impossible for her to forgive her stepmother for many years. Which was, in itself, hardly fair. It took two to tango, after all. In fact, it had only been once she'd left college and, after many false starts, had landed her dream job working for a public relations company in Seattle, that she'd begun to forgive Monika. She'd spent time looking after enough members of the entertainment industry — models, music stars, actors — that she realized now how toxic that world was and how easy it could be to stray from the straight and narrow path.

Rae had come along only a few months after her parents had formally separated; Monika's pregnancy the final slap in the face for herself and her mom. She'd been fourteen at the time, a volatile enough age in any case, and her relationship with her father had disintegrated, except for the summer and Christmas vacations. She honestly believed that without being forced to go on them, she'd have become completely estranged from her dad, the person she loved the most in all the world.

He'd supported her every ambition. Spoiled her, in fact. He'd paid for her to go to veterinary college but hadn't complained *too much* when she bailed out halfway through, seeking an easier way to make a living. She regretted that move now, in her late twenties, having spent half of the past decade soothing the fragile egos of the celebrity world's bottom feeders.

As she thought all this, she'd been running the cold water to clean the pipes, then filling the coffee machine and switching it on. With the aroma of roasted beans filling the kitchen and making its way into the living area, she dropped into the couch and took a deep breath. She was home.

\#

She was sitting in the rocking chair on the porch, wrapped in her favorite coat enjoying a double shot of Polar Ice, when Rae emerged and sat on the swing seat.

"I'm stuffed! What are you drinking?" she said, her breath steaming in the chill air.

"Vodka. And before you ask, no, you can't have any."

"I'm fifteen, you know!"

"Exactly. I brought some Bud with me. It's in the fridge."

"I can have one?"

"Sure."

Rae launched herself out of the swing seat, then grunted in pain.

"Be careful," Abby said. "Jeez, I shouldn't have to tell you. You're the one with C.P., not me."

Rae didn't respond, but she rubbed the back of her calf and limped into the house.

Emptying the glass, Abby reached for the bottle and poured herself a single. Rae's vulnerability made it a whole lot harder to maintain her hostility. She couldn't pretend she didn't care or that she wasn't horrified by the pain her sister had to endure when her body seized up. She'd be glad when Monika arrived, at least because she'd take of Rae's very personal care. A mix of medication, maturity and experience meant that she didn't have serious attacks as often as she once did, but it would be typical if she...

She heard a crash from inside the house and leaped out of the rocking chair so quickly she knocked her knees against the ancient oak and cursed as she ran through the door.

Rae was on the floor, arms locked to her side, vibrating as if she was experiencing her own private earthquake. Blood ran from her mouth and down the side of her face to pool on the varnished floorboards.

Crossing to where her sister lay, Abby dropped to her knees and grabbed a hand in hers. "Rae! Can you hear me?"

No response. The girl continued vibrating and Abby sat there helplessly, unable to even relax Rae's jaw enough to stop her biting the inside of her cheek. She put her arms around Rae and pulled her close, as if she could hug the rigidity away.

And then, quite suddenly, she relaxed, flopping so completely that Abby fell forward.

"Rae?"

"Hurts. I wet myself."

Abby looked down to the expanding pool. "It doesn't matter. You can clean it up later."

"Ha ha."

"Good, you're back. Is your medication in your bedroom?"

"Yeah."

"Then let's get you to bed."

"Shower first."

Abby was going to protest, but she relented. Rae was on the cusp of womanhood, and she didn't want her to feel humiliated. Besides, it would cut down on the laundry she'd have to do. "Okay. It'll have to be a cold one, the heating isn't up to temperature yet."

She helped her sister up, wincing at her obvious pain as she put weight on her legs. "That was a bad one," Rae said. "You should've let me have the vodka."

"Nice try, sister," Abby said, throwing her coat on the couch and pushing the back door shut against the cold as they passed it.

It took ten minutes to get her clean and into bed, and Abby watched as Rae went wearily through her pack, selecting some pain killers and anticonvulsant medication.

"You're going to have to wait for your Bud Light."

"It's okay, the meds will do."

"You've got enough for the holidays?"

"Yeah. I'm always prepared," she said, swallowing the last pill. "Ab?"

Abby took the glass of water from her. "Yeah?"

"Will you sit with me for a while? Until I'm asleep?"

"Sure. I'll just go get my drink."

She got up and made her way out to the porch to pick up the vodka. Before she went back inside, her cell went off in her pocket. She read the contact information before she put it to her ear.

"Hey, Dad. Yeah, we're here safe."

"*Oh, thank God.*"

The fear in his voice was obvious. "What is it?"

"*Are you inside the cabin? Both of you?*"

"Yeah, Rae had a seizure, but she's recovering now."

"*Listen to me, Abby. Don't go outside. Do you hear me? Stay in the cabin.*"

Abby froze at the back door. "What's going on, Dad?"

"*Just promise me you'll do as I say!*"

"Okay, okay!"

"*Good. We'll be there as soon as we—*"

"Dad? Daddy?" She took the phone from her ear and checked the display as she marched back inside. It was dead. But it had been fully charged. What a time for this to happen.

Moments later, the cabin lights went out. And, through the open door, she saw a rainbow dancing in the sky.

\#

"Rae. Rae!" She'd darted out to get her bottle of vodka and then run back in, feeling her way through the cabin to her sister's bedroom. As her eyes adjusted to the sudden darkness, she could make out a faint, gentle pulsing of color on the walls and in the mirror above the hearth. And the air outside seemed to be whistling.

"Wha...?"

Good grief, the medication had taken effect quickly. She cursed under her breath. Rae was usually as sharp as a tack and, besides that, the only other person here to talk to. But Rae needed to sleep, so Abby was left to her own devices for now.

She got up and moved to the living room. Power cuts weren't that unusual out here. They were at the far end of the distribution network and the last miles were generally on wooden poles. Chances were a tree had fallen and cut the line. Though that didn't explain why her father's signal had disappeared just before. Unless the cell masts were on their side of the outage. But that would mean it was widespread.

And what about her father's order to stay inside? He sounded desperate and, thinking back now, she was sure he'd been in a car at the time. Had he been heading this way? He wasn't due for another five days, but she was beginning to feel unsure about everything.

The first thing to do, she decided, was to get some light. She found the closet in the kitchen with the box marked "Power Cuts". She couldn't see the box, but she knew what it felt like, and knew what she'd written in Sharpie on the outside all those years ago.

The cardboard had softened over the years, and she put her hand under it to stop the contents falling out, then put it on the counter and felt around for a couple of candles and a box of matches. Within seconds, she had lit a candle and placed it inside a lantern, banishing the flickering rainbow, though she knew it was still out there. What could it be? Rae would have a theory, she felt sure. Rae! She had a cell!

Abby ran into her sister's room and found her phone on the bedside table. The display came on and, feeling a little guilty, Abby pressed Rae's finger to the sensor to unlock it. She swiped until she found their father's contact and pressed the green icon, her heart beating as she marched back to the kitchen. Nothing. She checked the display. *No network.*

"Dammit!" she hissed. She stood there for a moment, forcing herself to calm down. There was a generator in the shed that fed the cabin through an underground cable, but that would involve going outside, and she'd promised not to do that.

Could this be connected to the lights in the sky? With a stab, a thought struck her. Could it be a nuclear attack? Physics hadn't been her strong suit, but she imagined that if a hydrogen bomb went off, it would have some impact on the sky, wouldn't it?

Or perhaps she was jumping to conclusions. She'd spent so long around histrionic minor celebrities she'd become infected with their view of a world full of drama — generally centered around them if they were lucky.

Her father had told her to stay indoors, but what was there about being indoors that would protect them? Was it connected to the lights or, perhaps, it was some kind of insurrection? Or, just possibly ... could it be? The Rapture?

Most of her family wore their religion lightly, but she had an aunt who'd married into a fundamentalist group of some kind. She'd often spoken of the Rapture when she could get her to one side. She had a place down in Texas — more than 1,000 miles as the crow flies — and Abby had been banned from staying with her if her parents weren't also there, back before the divorce. She hadn't seen Aunt Grace for close on a couple of decades.

But if the colorful lights dancing in the sky weren't a portent of doom, she couldn't imagine what would be. She risked a look out of the window, squinting sideways through the treetops to the sky beyond to see the mesmeric pulsing, then withdrew herself as if simply looking at them might be enough to cause her harm.

She went back into the sitting room and slumped into the long couch, her gaze falling on the twin facing it. So many Christmases her with her closest family and, more often than not, other friends and family along for the ride. She had a bad feeling that she'd seen the last of these celebrations.

She sat in the dark, listening to the rustling of the trees outside and the distant wailing of sirens — at least, she assumed that was what she could hear — and said a silent prayer that her father would soon arrive. With him by her side, she could face anything. Even the end of the world.

8

Samuel & Ruth

Day 1: Pennsylvania

The man ran his hand along the furry flank of the cow and patted it. He didn't look up when the woman came in and kneeled beside him.

"Have you seen the sky?"

Samuel Gerber nodded. "Yes, but Judith here needs me. The calf is twisted."

"Can you help her?"

"I must. Will you hold her?"

"Of course."

Samuel smiled at his wife. He knew how lucky he was, though his parents disagreed. With his short mustache-less beard and plain shirt he was a typical member of the Mennonite community, whereas her dark skin made her stand out. But they were happy, and their faith was strong. And together, they would help this poor beast.

The cow bellowed as Samuel examined her by touch, his eyes roving around the inside of the barn. It was sturdy, though the roof leaked a little and yesterday's rain had soaked the bails of straw in the loft above his head, coming down in huge drops that had forced him to put his wide brimmed hat on again.

Then his gaze caught the half-open barn door and, above the muddy stockade outside, colorful bands of light shifting in the heavens. He thought he could hear the voices of angels mingled with the rain.

Ruth followed his eyes. "Do you recall *Luke 21:11*?"

"'fearful sights and great signs shall there be from heaven.'" he said.

"Don't you think this qualifies?"

He shrugged. "There's nothing I can do about it. It is either the Great Tribulation or it's not. But, either way, this cow needs me. I cannot believe a loving God would wish me to leave her to suffer, whatever is to come. Ah, I have the calf's head. Hold her, won't you?"

She moved to the animal's other end and wrapped one arm around its neck, stroking its face with the other.

Suddenly, the cow bellowed, lifting its head. It took all Ruth's weight to keep it down."

"Hold her! I nearly have it."

She hadn't been brought up on a farm, but she'd spent long enough in the community not to be squeamish, so she held on tight as the cow moaned, and, from the end where Samuel was working, she heard a sound like a wet towel being flung repeatedly against a wall. And then, finally, the high-pitched, frightened, wailing of the calf.

"Let her go," Samuel said, and Ruth gently released the mother so she could turn and, as the two humans stood back, greet her newborn.

"Thank God," Ruth said, putting her arm around her husband's waist. "Now, why don't you clean yourself up?"

Samuel shook his head. "They aren't out of danger yet. Judith lost a lot of blood, and the calf might have suffered oxygen starvation. I'll stay out here with them."

"Then I'll stay with you. I'll fetch some blankets and food for us. And some hot water bottles — it's going to be cold tonight."

He smiled as he watched her squeeze between the barn doors and run into the night. Beyond her, he could see the lights pulsing in the sky. He couldn't help but be a little frightened by the awe-inspiring spectacle, even as seen through the narrow gap. It would be prideful to imagine that he deserved to survive the tribulation and the judgement that would follow, but he was concerned for his wife. She was a good woman but had not had a conventional early childhood. Her father had abandoned the faith and she had been born to an African American mother who died when she was young. The father returned to the community only for long enough to hand her over to his parents. She'd been brought up by her grandparents as a good Mennonite, but her skin color had always marked her out from the others.

He sighed as he washed his hands clean. He had faith that the Lord would see her for what she was. He didn't believe that their childlessness after five years of marriage was a judgement. How could it be?

He'd dried his arm on a towel and was re-buttoning his cuff when she returned bearing blankets and a basket.

"Why are you looking at me like that?" she asked, smiling.

"I am giving thanks to the heavenly Father that he brought us together."

He climbed out of the pen and took her in his arms as she set her burden down.

"The lights are wonderful. Won't you come outside and look? And they're singing!"

In truth, he found them a little creepy, and that made him feel guilty. "I've seen enough through the door. We don't know what they mean, so perhaps we should be careful. And besides, it's cold and I would like to spend tonight wrapped in a blanket, in the arms of my beautiful wife. Did you bring the sauerkraut?"

She giggled and extracted the jar of pickled cabbage as they settled down to watch the animals.

\#

"Hello? I there anyone here?"

The voice woke Ruth first, and she gently touched Samuel's face to bring him around. "There's someone at the house."

After rinsing his face in cold water, Samuel checked on the cow and her calf, both of whom seemed to be content and well, and peered out of the barn. "It's Mrs. Proctor."

"Oh, really? Marcy's nice."

"For English."

He followed Ruth out of the barn, glancing across at the other barn where the remaining cattle had sheltered for the night. He felt guilty for not letting them out, but he'd do it once they'd seen what their visitor wanted.

Quite suddenly, Ruth began running toward the house.

"What's going on?" Sam called after her.

"She's hurt!"

Ruth's eyesight must have been much better than his, but he imagined the figure, who was moving around the house and looking in the windows, might be limping.

By the time he caught up with them, Ruth was examining Marcy Proctor's face. "How did you do this?"

"I think it must have been the lights in the sky. You know, last night. Or did you go to bed early and miss it?"

"We were tending a nursing cow," Samuel said. "Hello Mrs. Proctor."

Marcy smiled weakly and put out her hand. "Hi, Sam."

He suspected she did things like that deliberately to mock him and, by extension, his community. But he took her hand and nodded.

"Marcy's not well, Samuel," Ruth said, looking at him with obvious concern.

"Oh, I'm fine. It's Archer I'm worried about."

That was her husband — he worked in insurance out of an office in Pittsburgh. "What's wrong with him?"

"He's real sick. Came back last night covered in sores. Spent hours in the bathroom and now I can't get him out of bed. He's never missed a day's work before. I'm worried, Ruth. Will you come take a look at him?"

"Can't you call your doctor?"

"Samuel! Marcy is a neighbor, and she's asked for help. It's our duty to see what we can do."

Marcy nodded. "I couldn't get hold of the doctor — the phones are down. Power's gone too. Car won't start. So, I ran over there, but ... oh, Ruth, it's awful. There was a line a mile long outside the doctor's office, and some folks were just lying on the ground like they were dead. You've always been kind to me, so I couldn't think of anyone else to ask."

"Where are the children?"

"I've left them at the house."

Ruth turned to Sam. "Will you drive us over there in the buggy?"

Sam wanted to refuse — it was inappropriate that Ruth might see this man in his bed — but it would be even worse to have this conversation in front of an English woman. The idea of her going over there without him was completely out of the question, so he was left with no choice.

"I will. Please wait around the front of the house and I'll fetch the buggy."

He left them and harnessed up their horse. "You're warm," he mumbled, but then dismissed the thought — he'd been cold all night and the horse was only hot compared to him. He climbed up into the buggy and nudged it onto the road. His community wasn't as strict as the Old Order Amish, so he wasn't breaking any particular rule, especially as he was helping someone in need, but he didn't feel comfortable.

Marcy climbed into the back with Ruth, and he tickled the horse with the whip, then directed it along the road until they hit the edge of town.

"It's that one," Marcy said, leaning forward.

Neither Sam nor Ruth had been to her home, but it looked like most English ranch houses. There was a group of five along this part of the road, and Marcy's was the second. There was no sign of life in the first.

"Mommy!" A young girl emerged from the front door and ran down the path to gate in the white picket fence.

Marcy jumped out and embraced her daughter. "How's Daddy?"

"He doesn't answer me when I talk to him. I think he's asleep, but he sure looks sore."

Sam shook his head as he climbed down and stood beside Ruth.

"This is Kaitlin," Marcy said. "Darling, this is Mr. and Mrs. Gerber. Mrs. Gerber knows a lot about how to look after sick people."

"Hello. You've got a funny beard," Kaitlin said, looking up at Samuel. "Oh, of course, you're Amish, aren't you?"

"Don't be rude, Kaitlin!" Marcy snapped, pulling her daughter away and apologizing to the Gerbers.

"We're Mennonites," Samuel said, realizing that he was wasting his time. To English – especially English children – if you drove a buggy, had a beard but no mustache and wore plain clothes, then you were Amish.

They followed the woman into the house. It wasn't like theirs at all. Where they had sparse, functional furniture with area rugs over floorboards, every inch of the Proctor's house seemed to be full of possessions. Samuel wasn't entirely naïve; he knew this was typical of English houses, but he didn't know how they tolerated it. It seemed to press in on him from all sides.

A boy ran out and collided with Marcy. He looked around the same age as Kaitlin and looked at the visitors suspiciously. "Who are they, Mommy?"

"These are our neighbors, the Gerbers, Logan. Now, let me take a look at Daddy. Why don't you make Mr. Gerber a cup of coffee?"

"No, thank you," Samuel said, forcing a smile.

"Wouldn't you rather wait in the kitchen?"

Sam shook his head. "I'm sorry, but I can't allow my wife to be in the company of another man without a guardian."

For a moment, it seemed that Marcy would argue, but pain flickered in her face, she rubbed her temples and then opened an internal door. "I'll go in first," she said.

Sam and Ruth stood outside the bedroom, each taking in the strange environment, exchanging disbelieving glances. Until Ruth finally felt compelled to speak. "It is not for us to judge."

"Indeed," Samuel whispered. "But it is difficult to understand how anyone can live like this."

"I expect they would say the same about our house."

He smiled at her wisdom.

The door opened and Marcy appeared. "He's unconscious. Will you look at him?"

With a glance at Samuel, Ruth smiled and moved inside.

Samuel remained at the door, but he could see enough of the room to know that the man in the bed was no threat to his wife. He began a silent prayer for God to ease Mr. Proctor's passing as, though he was no medical expert, he could sense the shadow of death here.

When, after ten minutes or so, Ruth emerged again, she ushered Sam and Marcy outside the house. "I'm sorry, Marcy, but your husband needs the hospital, urgently. There's nothing I can do for him."

"But I can't call an ambulance! And my car doesn't work, even if I could get him in it."

"Marcy?"

They turned to see a woman walking unsteadily toward them. "Emma? Oh, my God! You've got it too?"

Marcy ran to the woman and helped her into a plastic chair on the porch.

"John ... John's dead, Marcy. John's dead!" She began sobbing into her inflamed hands. "It's those damn lights in the sky, I swear. They gave me the creeps and I told him not to look for long, but everyone was out in their yards. It was like a party. He was as sick as a dog, but I thought it could be the drink. When I went into his room this morning, I knew straightaway he was ... gone."

"You poor woman," Ruth said. "And you look sick yourself."

The woman looked at her out of bloodshot eyes. "I am. And I just don't know what to do. I can't leave John there; he needs to be ... taken care of. I went see the Garcias, but they're sick too. And my phone isn't working, so I can't tell my son what's ... what's happened."

She began sobbing again, and as Ruth comforted her, Samuel took Marcy to one side. "Mrs. Proctor, is there anywhere people can gather? Any empty properties?"

"Yes, the Halsworths have moved west. It's all boarded up."

"Any furniture?"

"Not as far as I know. Why do you ask?"

Samuel rubbed his bearded chin absent-mindedly. "Do you know anything about the lights in the sky last night? Was there any news coverage on the television?"

"Not really. They showed a few photos and phone videos, but the network went down almost immediately. Archer only just made it home before the power went out. Do you think it's God's judgement?"

Looking along the road at the house she'd indicated, Samuel sighed. "I can't say for certain what's happened. Ruth and I were tending a cow who was giving birth, but I could see the lights through the barn door. Scripture talks of the Great Tribulation before our Lord returns, but I am not learned enough to say if this is that. Satan is the master of deceit."

As he listened to the sound of his own voice, he felt a growing sense of what he must do. It would be prideful to assume it was the Holy Spirit, but he was glad of some direction. He had a feeling that things in the world would never be the same again, and what he did now would be judged when the time came.

"There isn't much we can hope to achieve, Mrs. Proctor, but we will do what we can. We will help your family and those who come to you for aid. But, to do that, we will need help. I will seek it from our neighbors."

Ruth, who'd gotten to her feet, touched his arm. "You're right, of course, Samuel. What should we do while we wait for you?"

"Open up that house and get the sick inside — those who can be moved, that is. Salvage any camp beds. If we are to tend them, they must be gathered together."

"You're leaving me here?"

"I don't have any choice. I'm going to ride over to the Millers' place and see if they'll help."

She took his hand and squeezed it. He wanted to kiss her, but that wouldn't be seemly in public. "Will you give my greetings to Sarah?" she asked.

"I will. And I'll be back as soon as I can. Sarah and her daughters will help tend the sick."

"Will you bring Amos and his son?"

"Yes. And I'll bring spades. Sadly, I believe we will have much digging to do today."

#

The Millers had a farm on the edge of town. Larger than Samuel's, it had been in their family for generations and was currently run by Amos Miller and his son David.

"Come on, boy," Samuel called, flicking the reins. Rosh was a chestnut gelding who'd been faithfully transporting the Gerbers to and from meetings for five years now, but Samuel was worried about him. When he'd returned to the buggy, he'd found that the horse was running a temperature. Normally, he'd have left the horse in his stable, but these weren't normal times, so he'd driven him as fast as he dared.

The Miller farm was no more than a quarter mile away when, quite suddenly, Rosh snorted, his head rearing up, and he collapsed sideways, landing on the left hand trace and pinning it. Reflexively, Samuel jumped from the buggy as it flipped sideways, then twisted in the air, coming down on its side with the sound of splintering wood.

Samuel landed on his backside in the grass by the side of the road, then leaped up and ran across to where the stricken horse lay. He knew Rosh was dead before he reached him. Blood ran from his nostrils and Samuel could see sores developing around its mouth and eyes. He held the horse's head and wept for his friend, looking back and forth along the road, desperately hoping for any sign of help.

The only help would come when he made it to the Millers' farm, so he wiped his tears away and retrieved his hat from where it had landed in the grass, then, without looking back, he ran along the road, hoping to find friendly faces.

There it was! A light rain was falling as he jogged, his mind whirling as he pressed the hat to his head. Poor Rosh. The stable had a sort of courtyard which the beast used to get a breath of air. Did he look up at the night sky and wonder what the lights were? Even as they were killing him. If it was God's doing, why would he kill a faithful animal?

But it wasn't for him to question the wisdom of the Father. All he could do now was to help as he could in what he increasingly believed was the prelude to the Tribulation. People needed his help and English were also God's children, so he would do what he could.

Then he rounded the corner and headed onto the lane leading to the farm. To his right, he could see the farmhouse emerging from behind the line of trees that lent privacy to the family from passersby on the road.

He knew, before he reached the house, that something was terribly wrong. Something lay on the ground in front of the house, beside a picnic bench that he'd often sat on in happier times.

Something or someone. More than one. The family. Amos Miller lay with his arms around his wife as if looking up at heaven. But his eyes weren't moving. Beside them lay their son and two daughters, all dressed in their best Sunday clothes. Small suitcases lay at their feet, as if they'd been ready for a journey before being struck down ... by what? Surely they hadn't lain there looking into the heavens even as those very lights killed them. Like moths to the flame.

"Oh, Amos," Samuel said, kneeling beside his friend and closing his eyes. "Did you wait to be taken up to be beside our Lord? Maybe you succeeded. Who am I to tell?"

And, as he went from one family member to the other, he wondered how many tragedies like this there had been. Perhaps the faith of the Millers had been rewarded, but he hoped that Sarah Miller had used her knowledge of herbs to ease their pain. He stood and said a short prayer over them, then dragged tarps out of the barn and laid them over the bodies.

Would the lights return tonight? Or were they up there now, hidden by the daylight? Was he dying even as he stood here and prayed?

He couldn't know. It was in the hands of God. All he could do for now was to remain faithful to his promise to return to his wife and help as he could.

He went to the stable and found a black mare, taking it round to where their cart stood. Then, he piled every digging tool he could find into the back and drove down the hill, past the temporary mound hiding the bodies. He made an oath to return to give them a proper burial and then, as he left the farm, he wondered how many promises he would make today, and how many he would be able to keep.

9

Elijah

Day 2: Glendale, L.A.

It felt as though he were underwater, the pressure building up as he struggled, in vain, to draw air into his lungs.

"You're okay."

He didn't recognize the voice and flailed out as consciousness seeped back and along with it came the pain. Elijah Wade opened his eyes: he couldn't see!

And then something slid from his head, and he made out the amber-lit face of someone looking down at him.

"B ... Becky?"

"Yeah, it's me."

And suddenly full awareness flooded back. He sat up, instantly regretting it as his head felt as though it were being squeezed by a giant hand.

"My piece."

"It's here."

He felt the reassuring weight of his Colt. "You ran off."

"I came back. I heard you collapse."

"How long?"

"I dunno, since last night. This is the first time you've made any sense since then. Who's Kelly?"

Wade adjusted himself so he was upright, taking it slowly to keep the migraine under control. "My daughter."

"Yeah, I figured. You want some drugs?"

"You know I'm a cop."

She chuckled. "I mean pain killers. That sicko's got a closet-full."

Wade felt his head, then his fingers touched something uneven and sore on his neck.

"Came up yesterday. My grandma used to have them on her legs."

Hauling himself to his feet, Wade waited for his head to stabilize, then staggered into the bathroom, followed by Becky who held up a candle so he could see himself. The only other light came from the cracks between the drapes, closed against the nightmare outside.

He cursed under his breath. It was as if he were looking through a mirror in time and seeing himself two decades in the future. Even in the yellow light of the candle he looked pale and half dead. He leaned back to look at his neck. A weeping sore sat there like a particularly malignant hickey. He didn't dare explore it with his fingers. "What is this?"

"I don't know, but you're not the only one I've seen with marks like that."

"You've been outside?"

She nodded. "Stayed here all night with you, then went out when it quietened down."

They moved back into the living room. The drapes were closed against the night, but there was no sound from outside. "What did you see?"

Shaking her head, she sat on a wooden chair, deliberately avoiding the armchair. "Dead people, just lying there. And I could see fires farther away. Someone called out to me, but I ran back here."

Wade sighed, taking the Advil with a mug of water. "Well, I appreciate you looking after me."

"You saved my life. If you hadn't have come, I'd be ... I'd still be hogtied in that room waiting for that ... him to come back. He told me he'd killed other girls before me, and he'll kill more after."

"He won't. He's locked up at the station."

"Detective?"

"Call me Elijah."

"Elijah. What's happened to the world?"

He could feel the migraine coming again. "I don't know. Maybe an attack. Nukes, perhaps. I guess the power's still out?" He pulled the cell out of his pocket, but it was dead.

"Yeah. I guess I was lucky to be locked up in a room with loads of candles," she said, sarcastically. "Look, Elijah, what are we gonna do?"

He saw the pleading in her face. She was only here because she had nowhere else to go, only with him because she had no one else to be with. "I don't know, Becky, I really don't. Right now, I've got to rest. If it is a nuclear attack of some sort, then I guess I took a dose of radiation. Nothing I can do right now. I need ... to ...."

#

It was darker in the serial killer's living room when he awoke for the second time. He couldn't see any cracks of light, and only a single candle flickering on the low table.

"Becky?"

She emerged from the armchair, uncurling like a cat. "You okay?"

He put his hand on to his temple. "Better."

"At least you're not getting any worse. I've been thinking about ghosts."

"What?"

"I mean, how many has he killed here?"

Wade pulled himself upright, his mind working well enough that he could, at last, think about anything beyond his immediate condition. This young woman had been sitting there, in Silas Lynch's chair, while her rescuer lay helpless. Good grief, he could only imagine how her thoughts had wandered. "He didn't kill here. Our profile said he had a fetish for hygiene, and all the victims were found in remote locations. He took them out of the home, so it remained clean. Though I don't know how he managed that without the neighbors noticing."

"So, no one died here?"

"Not as far as I know."

She shook her head while rubbing distractedly at her scalp. "Then why do I hear them? His victims?"

"What?"

He was alert now, looking around as if he could identify the source of these noises.

"Moaning. Couldn't tell where it was coming from, but I've been sat here so long, I thought maybe it was my imagination. Then I thought it could be a ghost."

"I don't hear anything."

"No, it comes and goes. Do you want anything to eat or drink?"

The thought of eating made him suddenly nauseous, and his head swam as he lay back down. "Some water, please."

He took the water and, in the end, accepted a cookie. He knew he couldn't stay here, but, for now, he didn't have the strength to leave.

"Thank you for staying with me," he said.

"You said that already."

He gestured vaguely with his hand. "But you must have been scared, hearing those sounds. You didn't run out on me."

She fell back into the armchair. "Like I said, I owe you. And I figure, once you're better, you're a good person to keep close, being a cop."

"I've got my own business, Becky."

"Your daughter?"

"Yeah. But right now, I'm going nowhere." And, as he eased himself up onto his elbows, he heard it. "There it is!"

Becky leaped up. "I'm not going crazy!"

"It's coming from the apartment above," Wade said. He had a bad feeling about this.

"Do you think he owns the one upstairs, too? Maybe there's somebody up there! Come on!"

Wade didn't need the encouragement because he suspected she was right. He got to his feet, then swayed, steadied by Becky's hand grabbing his. Jeez, he hated feeling so weak. He needed to rest up, but the moan he heard spoke of desperation, and if he ignored it, he could be too late. Besides, if he didn't go, he knew Becky would. And she'd been through enough already.

Picking up his 1911, he slipped on his shoes and made his way to the door. Boy, his legs felt weak. "Have you got a weapon?"

Becky nodded and lifted her arm to reveal a kitchen knife.

"Good, just don't use it unless you absolutely have to, okay?"

"Scared Ima gonna stab you in the back?"

He couldn't resist smiling at that. "A little. But no, you've been through enough already. And I'm trained for this."

She returned his smile, though he could see how nervous she was. Nervous and exhausted — if not physically, then certainly emotionally.

He nodded, then pulled the chain on the front door across and opened it a crack. He scanned the darkness. He must have been asleep for hours, the only light source the fires that must still be burning throughout the city.

Pressing his ear to the gap, he listened. Nothing close, as far as he could tell. When he filtered out his breathing, he could hear the occasional shout, of sounds of glass shattering and things falling in the distance. No gunshots yet.

He inched the door further open and looked left and right, then past it until he was sure there was no movement nearby. Maybe a fourth of the windows opposite showed signs of life: candles flickering behind closed drapes, but only on the upper floor of the apartment block opposite, which mirrored the one they were in.

"You sure you don't want to wait here?" he whispered.

She shook her head, eyes wide for emphasis.

Wade snuck around the door and flattened himself against the outer wall. Lynch's apartment was the last one on the first floor, so it was only a few feet to the stairwell. Wade gazed up at the night sky. No sign of the aurora, but no stars either, and he doubted the clouds would be an effective shield against the radiation if the rainbow was in the sky above them. So, they had to get inside as quickly as possible. He felt as though he was recovering but knew that another dose of radiation would probably finish him off.

Skirting around the corner, he looked up the aluminum stairs. At the top, there would be a walkway that took residents along the front of the second-floor apartments. But he was going to the one immediately above, beyond the dark opening at the top of the stairs.

He hauled himself up the first few steps, treading as lightly as he could, keeping his eyes fixed firmly on the top of the stairs, ears straining for any sounds. As they got higher, the background noise grew louder, and he felt a breeze tingling his cheeks.

Stopping halfway up, he took a deep breath. He felt as though he was at Everest's base camp, contemplating the climb to the peak. And he found himself craving a smoke even as he cursed his nicotine habit for robbing him of a lung capacity he could really do with right now.

Before Becky could ask him how he was, he started climbing again, holding onto the rail and using his arms to propel him upward.

As they reached the top, he glanced along the balcony. More apartments had lights on up here, but there was no sign of any movement.

He stood in the darkness under the balcony roof, leaning against the bricks and waiting for Becky to reach him.

"Remember," he whispered as he caught his breath, "don't use the knife unless you absolutely have to."

"I got the message, stop patronizing!"

Wade leaned his head against the door and listened. He couldn't hear anything, and he couldn't afford to wait. Standard procedure would be to announce his presence and give those inside a chance to let him in without any violence. But these weren't standard times. He reckoned, having examined the lock on Silas Lynch's apartment, that he could kick the door open, eventually, and assuming he had the strength, but then he'd kiss goodbye to any chance of surprise.

"There's someone in there," Becky said.

"What are you doing?"

"Getting cold, that's what. I figured you'd blow the lock off, or something."

"That only works in the movies," he said. "Come on, we're going to have to kick it down."

He leaned back, holding onto the wall as he lifted his boot, his Colt 1911 held upright.

Then the door swung open. "Who the hell are you?"

A young man stood there, waving a small revolver in his hand, his finger on the trigger as he saw Wade's much larger weapon.

It was shoot or be shot.

But Becky lunged forward, grabbed the young man's gun and wrenched it out of his hands.

"Hey! What the f—"

"Stand still!" Wade snapped. "She just saved your life. Now, step back and let us in."

"He's only a kid, Elijah."

"A kid with a gun." Wade had seen too many people — cops and civilians — killed by minors. Now he could be seen clearly, the young man was obviously younger than he'd appeared. A yellow T-shirt failed to cover his huge belly and he stood there, hands in the air, as crumbs tumbled out of sight. Ten years older and he'd be a textbook loner killer. Maybe he'd just started young. Kids grow up so quickly these days, Wade thought, his mind inevitably turning to his daughter even as the boy retreated backward into the room.

"He's police," Becky said, glancing at Elijah with obvious concern. "Who have you got in here?"

Wade kept his gun raised and skirted around Becky until he was inside, his weapon scanning this carbon copy layout.

"What you talkin' about?"

"We heard moaning from this apartment," Elijah said. "And it didn't sound like it was you." He made his way toward the door to the second bedroom. In Lynch's apartment, this had been the one with the wardrobe and fake wall where he'd kept his victims.

"Please don't go in there!" the boy said, hands outstretched. "You don't understand!"

He made a move toward Becky, but she simply stepped back and raised the knife threateningly. "Keep back, you son of a —"

"Please! Don't! You'll only make it worse!"

That was enough for Wade. He grabbed the youth in one hand, pushing him toward the door with his gun pressed into the ribs. "Open the damn door!"

The boy was weeping softly as his trembling hands turned the handle and the door swung open.

"Oh my God!"

"Becky! Wait!"

But it was too late. She was inside, and Wade couldn't move without letting his prisoner go.

There, on the bed, lay a young woman. She was large-framed and lay on her side, her long hair slicked to her head and almost completely obscuring her face.

Her hands and legs were tied together, and a belt wrapped around the base of the metal-framed bed, giving her no chance to escape. She had a leather gag in her mouth that accounted for the strange moans they'd heard from the apartment downstairs.

"Please! Leave her!"

"You scum! How long has she been here?" Wade said, watching as Becky began to untie the girl, who seemed entirely unresponsive."

"Two ... two years."

"What? You've kept her tied up for two years?"

"You don't understand. You mustn't let her go."

"Like hell I don't," Becky said, removing the gag and stroking the hair from the girl's face.

Wade looked from the girl to the boy and back again. The resemblance was unmistakable.

The girl moaned and her eyes flicked open, looking at the strangers with obvious terror.

"Cody ... what's ... what's ..."

"We're here to get you out," Becky said. "You're safe now."

And then Wade saw it. Beside the bed, empty bottles of meds. Topamax, Tegretol, Zonegran. He cursed under his breath and let the youth go. "She's epileptic," he said. "And she's his sister."

Becky looked up from the bed and looked from one to the other and then to Wade. "Oh my God. What the hell were you thinking?" she said, looking up at the boy.

"No ... no meds."

She went to get up and the boy moved toward her, only for her to wave him away. "I'm okay. Just need to calm down."

"You've kept her restrained in here for two years?" Wade said, turning to the young man.

He shrugged. "We didn't have a choice. It was make rent or buy meds."

Wade almost asked him why he didn't have medical insurance, then remembered where he was. Anyone who could afford insurance wouldn't be living somewhere like this.

"I work in a grocery store, and I couldn't leave Shelley on her own in case she had a seizure."

"So, you tied her up?"

"I told him to," the girl said. "He's a good brother and he got meds when he could, though he never told me how. But they've run out. Even Cody can't keep me safe if I have a bad one."

"And then those lights came, and people are goin' crazy, and I can't go out anyways."

Wade shook his head. "You can't restrain someone for hours like this!"

"You think I like it? She's my sister, man! But what can I do if she swallows her tongue, or hurts herself when she has a seizure?"

"You okay, Elijah? You look awful pale," Becky said, looking up at him.

He swayed a little, then went into the living room and dropped onto the couch, his skin crawling as something crunched under him. Becky appeared beside him. He felt weak, and even his mind seemed to be moving in slow-mo. "Give me a minute. I'll be alright." Then he looked up at the boy, who was standing in the doorway to the bedroom, drew in a deep breath, and marshaled his strength "Come on, Cody. We better go shopping."

10

Hannah

Hannah was woken by a sense of pressure and movement. She snorted and tried to move, but her head hurt like hell, and she collapsed into the soft bed.

"It's me, Shane. I'm just checking for any sores. Sorry, but you weren't awake to ask your permission."

She yawned, then dug a finger into her temple. "Where am I?"

"You're in Kuchinsky's quarters. You collapsed on the stairs, and this was the nearest place I could put you. I think you're going to be okay, for now at least. Nobody else has woken up once they fell asleep."

She felt full awareness making an unwelcome return. "Priti," she gasped.

"Yeah. Look, you did the right thing, got it? I reckon it was delayed shock that made you collapse, as much as the radiation."

Hannah pulled herself into a sitting position. "Kuchinsky?"

"Dead. Took himself outside, which was good of him."

She looked at the photo on the bedside table. A man and his family, smiling.

"How long was I out for?"

"Twelve hours or so. It's tomorrow now." He handed her a bottle of water. "Get yourself hydrated and take another iodine tablet."

He went to get up, but she grabbed his arm. "How many ... survived?"

He shook his head, looking downcast. "There's me and there's you. Bixby's still with us, but he's sick as hell."

"That's it?"

"Yeah. I had to help some of them, God help me."

She looked into his eyes and saw a man existing beyond his limits. She even felt a little fear as she held his trembling arm.

"I'll get up and help. You need some rest."

"No, you've got to get better. Leave it to me."

"Shane."

"I said, I'll handle it!"

With that, he swung away, striding out of the room and pulling it shut behind him.

She lay there for a few minutes, the vice squeezing her temples showing no signs of easing. She could stay in bed — Kuchinsky's bed — and recover for a while. Or she could get her butt out and help Shane. However little she could do in practice, he needed to know she wasn't a lightweight. But she felt like one, that was for sure. She'd lived a pampered existence, compared with the vast majority of people on the planet, and her complaints of having to rough it in the container bedrooms below rang hollow in her mind now.

Hannah heaved her legs over the side of the bed. She ran her hands over her bare knees, checking for any sores, but her deep coffee colored skin was unblemished. That, at least, was a good sign, but as she got to her feet, she swayed, thrusting out a hand to steady herself. She had to remember that she was on an upper floor — if she wanted to come back to this room, she'd have to be strong enough to climb the stairs.

She found the cell on the bedside cabinet but wasn't at all surprised that it was dead. Whatever the nature or cause of the radiation that had decimated the observatory, it had also functioned as an electromagnetic pulse, frying all unshielded electronics.

She thought about the container bedrooms — they had been built into the rocks and were sheltered by the observatory above them, so some of the instruments and devices down there ought to work. But that was for tomorrow, right now, she had to get herself dressed and lend a hand.

She found Shane on the ground level, kneeling beside someone lying on the floor. He'd spread a coat over the person's body but was almost as still as the person he was watching over.

His head snapped around as he heard her approach, and she saw utter exhaustion in his red-rimmed eyes. "I told you to stay in bed," he snapped, though without much energy.

"Yeah, well, I've never been very good at doing what I'm told. Oh, it's Bixby."

She only knew it was him by his distinctive Van Dyke beard, emerging incongruously from a mass of red, inflamed flesh. Mercifully, most of his skin was covered by the coat, but his hand lay on his chest, trembling.

"I've given him morphine, almost enough to kill him. Came down here to finish the job, but I can't do it, Han."

She put her hand on his shoulder. "Go get some sleep, I'll look after him."

"The others need burying," Shane said, casting his eyes lazily over the unmoving forms on the polished floor and couches of the reception area.

"Not right now. We'll handle it later. Get some sleep."

He looked as though he was going to argue, but then shut his mouth, glanced at the unconscious Bixby and got clumsily to his feet.

"Where are you going?" Hannah asked as he made his way toward the stairs to the upper floors.

He continued walking but shook his head. "Don't want to go down there."

She understood. Gravity had dictated that most of the sick people had gone down to the container bedrooms and, even if his room was unoccupied, Shane obviously didn't want to sleep surrounded by the dead.

She watched him struggle up the stairs until he disappeared into one of the bedrooms on the upper level.

Then something touched her hand. She swallowed the shriek as she snatched her arm back, then looked down.

"I know. Horrific, I'm sure."

"Doctor Bixby."

She took his hand again, mastering her fear and disgust.

"Elliott. Formalities are meaningless, are they not?"

She nodded but found nothing to say.

"Shane tells me you were the one who checked the observations."

"Too late."

"Not your fault. Not your shift. These people ... died because of ... me."

"No!"

"I am a scientist, but I let the pretty lights ... distract me."

She squeezed his hand. "Try to relax. Do you want some more morphine?"

"Soon. But I wish to discuss a theory with you."

"What?"

"It is what we do, isn't it?"

"But ..." She looked down at the ruined face, and the tiny smile on the cracked, sore lips. He needed this. "Sure, of course."

He took a deep breath as they sat on the floor in otherwise complete silence. "You must establish the source, Doctor ..."

"Hannah."

"Hannah. It is not manmade. Too powerful. Perhaps aliens, you never know. Maybe their first act on encountering us ... is to sterilize the planet." He chuckled, then rocked with convulsions, before subsiding again in obvious pain. "No, please listen. Let us assume it is natural."

"But, in that case, why didn't we detect it long ago?"

"That is what you must discover. The bomb does not go off ... until you light ... the fuse."

She sat back on her haunches, looking out through the open door to the courtyard where most of her colleagues received a lethal dose. "The solar wind? That would explain why the lights resemble an aurora."

"Perhaps. It is ... vital that you understand."

She sighed. "I can't believe I'm asking this, as a scientist, but why, exactly?"

"Perhaps it can be predicted."

Her jaw dropped. Until now, she'd assumed that this had been a single, catastrophic, event. What if it were repeated? She didn't doubt that millions, possibly billions, had been irradiated on the previous night. Maybe at lower altitudes, the effects might not have been so near-instantaneous, but she couldn't believe that a few thousand feet of air would make that much difference. Right now, a large portion of humanity was either dead or dying. The longer the lights persisted as the Earth turned, the greater the catastrophe. But how much worse would it be for humankind to survive, as a species, only for a second event to deliver the coup de grace? And, unless mankind was going to become like HG Wells' morlocks and live entirely underground, they would need a way of predicting when it was unsafe to go outside.

"Good," the man at her feet said, his voice coming in shorter and shorter gasps. "Your scientific curiosity has returned. There is much you must do, simply to survive the coming days, Hannah, but you must also remain what you are: a scientist. The future of our species — the future of all species — depends upon it. I suggest you begin by consulting the register of supernovae. You may need to go back some centuries. Now, if you will leave me the morphine, I think I would like to sleep."

"Let me," she said, opening the bottle.

He gripped her wrist between trembling fingers. "No. You are already burdened enough. I can do this for myself.

Good luck, Hannah."

She wrapped her hand around his, then gave him the open bottle and a bottle of water. The crazy thing was that she didn't know where she should go, so she wandered aimlessly, until she simply had to escape the feeling of being surrounded by the dead. In the end, she climbed the stairs to Kuchinsky's room, legs cramping as she reached the top, and fell on the bed beside Shane.

He wasn't there when she woke up, and she had no memory of being disturbed. As far as she could tell, she'd gone to sleep and then instantly awoken — except that the sun had disappeared, and her headache had lessened a little.

The emergency generator was on, so she was able to find her way down the stairs safely enough. There was no sign of Doctor Bixby, but, as far as she could tell, none of the bodies had moved.

She couldn't find Shane down here, but then she felt a cold breeze on her face and noticed that the outer doors were open. A sudden burst of adrenaline banished the last vestiges of sleep as she hurried down the final steps and ran to the door, standing on the threshold and looking up.

The sky was dark. Perfect conditions for astronomical observations — which was why the cluster of observatories was here, after all— but no astronomers. Except one.

"Shane!"

He was standing a little way from the main dome, feet in the volcanic soil, gazing up. He kept his eyes to the heavens as he sensed her approach. "I buried Bixby. Found him dead when I came round. You gave him the morphine?"

"Yeah."

"So beautiful," he said, looking up at the broad band of the Milky Way. "No sign of the aurora, so I think we're safe for now."

"Bixby told me to investigate, otherwise we won't know if it'll happen again."

Shane nodded, then gestured at a pile of dark earth a few yards away. "It was bloody hard to dig, and I couldn't go as deep as I'd like. We'll have to find somewhere else for the others."

"I can't believe no one else survived."

"Not here, anyway. Who knows about the other observatories? Maybe they weren't as careless."

Hannah put her hand on his shoulder. "I guess we'd better get digging, then. Our friends deserve to be buried properly, however long it takes. Best to do it while we can see the sky."

"You think the lights'll be back?"

"I don't know, but let's at least make a start while we can."

She felt a sudden hunger, then realized she hadn't eaten in twenty-four hours. She'd need to overcome her shame at this basic human need, feeling as though she should be in a period of mourning when such trivialities shouldn't even be considered. But, if she was going to spend the night digging, she needed calories. She was one of only two human beings that she knew, for a fact, had survived, which made her health and fitness a top priority. She could work on discovering what had happened once the all too human job of burying her friends had been completed. For now, she had digging to do.

Hannah made her way through into the storage area in the center of the observatory, buried beneath the volcanic sand in a cellar constructed from yet another pair of shipping containers. The emergency lights worked down here, and, to her relief, she found no dead bodies waiting for her. The weather conditions on Mauna Kea saw the observatory sometimes cut off for a week or two at a time, so she knew there was a store of dried and canned foods. One thing they didn't have to worry about was lack of food, at least not for some time.

She found some packets of chocolate wafers, ate one then and there, then brought an armful up from the cellar and left them on the reception desk. Hannah briefly wondered where Eve had been when the lights had appeared. Eve Kai was the administrative manager — it was often said that the observatory revolved around her as the Earth orbits the sun — but she often returned home to be with her family, so perhaps she'd been away for the party. But then, she would still have seen the lights from Hilo. Perhaps she'd had the good sense to keep her family sheltered.

Hannah ate another chocolate bar and followed it with a bottle of water, keeping her eyes fixed on the empty swivel chair behind the reception desk and not on the unmoving figures. She was glad of the fresh breeze blowing up the volcano and in through the open door. But she didn't allow herself to dwell on what she was about to do, or on the overall situation. Focus on one minute, one action at a time. Her instinct told her this was the best chance she had of keeping a grip on her sanity.

"Right, let's get going," Shane said, appearing alongside her and helping himself to a chocolate bar. "Who do you we begin with?"

"Priti," Hannah said. Her burial would take the greatest toll, so it was best to get it done as quickly as possible. "We just need to get something to move her on."

They found a low equipment trolley in the generator room and gently laid the bundle of clothes that had once been Hannah's friend on it. She only knew how tightly she'd been clenching her jaw when they finally made it out into the fresh air and onto the paved path that wound around the observatory and down the side of the mountain.

Shane had found two spades which he was carrying as she wheeled Priti's body along. "Here, this'll do. Let me just dig a test pit, make sure it's deep enough."

She watched as the Australian made a spade-width hole that he extended backwards as he deepened the end.

"That'll do," Hannah said as she began maneuvering the trolley off the path until it was in front of the trench. Together, they widened it, saying nothing and accompanied by the sounds of their spades digging and the occasional grunt of effort.

Finally, it was time. Hannah quickly realized she would have to get into the grave in order to gently ease Priti inside, and she had a moment of claustrophobic terror as she felt herself closed in on all sides, looking up to see Shane's head dimly visible against the star field behind. All it would take would be to begin backfilling the trench and she'd be buried alive.

But his hand reached down and she gripped it, climbing on the handle of the trolley and hauling herself over the edge of the trench.

"You gotta be careful, Han. That lot could come down on you and I wouldn't be able to dig you out in time. Jeez, do you know how precious you are?"

She took in several deep breaths and wiped her hands on her jeans to clean them, then helped Shane shovel the loose soil into the soul.

"I should say something," Hannah said, as Priti disappeared into the dark earth.

"What? She wasn't religious, as far as I know."

Hannah stood beside the grave, searching for inspiration. Then, out of nowhere, she found herself chanting:

This truth within thy mind rehearse
that, in a boundless universe
is boundless better, boundless worse.
Think you this mold of hopes and fears
Could find no statelier than his peers
In yonder hundred million spheres?

"That's beautiful," Shane said.

"I think it's Tennyson."

They stood together beside the grave and said goodbye to their friend in utter silence.

And then they heard the sound of clapping emerge from the night behind them.

11

Abby & Rae

Day 2: California

"Abby, wake up."

Her eyelids had stuck together. Had she been crying?

"Did you sleep out here?"

Abby forced her eyes open and pushed herself up. She'd fallen asleep on the couch, her mind finally shutting down in the small hours. "Yeah."

"Too much vodka?"

"No."

"The power's still out."

Abby rubbed her eyes and looked up at her sister who was dressed in a *Star Trek: Discovery* onesie. Her face looked drawn and puffy. "You look like I feel."

"It's the meds. I'll be a bit groggy today. Pity the power's not on, I could do with curling up with Netflix."

Then it all came back to Abby. "We've got to talk, but first I need a coffee."

"I'll make it. I could do with a shot of caffeine."

As her sister clattered around the kitchen, Abby wandered to the back door and looked out. It all seemed normal enough.

She heard the clicking of the stove-top gas lighter and glanced back at where her sister was stifling a yawn as she lifted the pot onto the hob. Rae was at the awkward age between childhood and becoming an adult, a distinction further blurred by her insistence on a Peter Pan hairstyle, and her tomboyish range of interests.

Abby chided herself for thinking in such sexist terms, but Rae was more at home with technology than most girls her age. This shared interest had drawn Rae and their father close, especially in recent years, and Abby was self-aware enough to know that this was one source of her remaining resentment toward her sister.

It wasn't Rae's fault that she took after their father whereas Abby was more like her mother. It wasn't Rae's fault that she was super-smart or that she was immature for her age. And it wasn't Rae's fault that she'd been born with cerebral palsy.

"It's taking ages," she said, looking across at where Abby stood in the doorway.

Moving across to the stove, Abby got a couple of cups out of the closet. "It's best to boil the water first, then pour it into the bottom of the coffee maker. Then you add the coffee to the chamber and put it on the stove."

"You could have told me," Rae said.

"How was I supposed to know you hadn't made it before?"

Rae shrugged. "I think it's nearly done now. Smells awesome."

"Yeah. Look, Rae, something bad's happened. I'm not sure what, but I haven't heard from Dad since last night."

They took the coffee out onto the veranda.

Rae sat down and looked out at the forest. A fine mist hung in the air, shrouding the tops of the conifers that surrounded the cabin. The morning was perfectly still, and the only sound was the dripping of water from the roof.

"Last night, when you'd gone to sleep, there was an aurora."

"Really? Awesome!"

"I have a bad feeling that it was connected to the power going out, and our cells not working."

Rae cupped her mug in both hands and sipped at the coffee. "Auroras are caused by charged particles from the sun interacting with the upper atmosphere. I suppose if there was a massive solar eruption, it might have caused an EMP."

"A what?"

"Electromagnetic Pulse. It can wipe out anything with a chip if it's powerful enough and the electronics aren't shielded,"

Abby watched her sister speak, then added, "Is the power related to how colorful it is? I mean it was like every color was up there."

"Auroras are green."

"Not this one."

"Then it wasn't an aurora."

Abby shrugged. "It sure looked like one. But, anyway, it has to be connected, surely?"

"I guess. And it would explain why we haven't heard from Dad. Oh, no!"

"What?"

She turned in her chair to face Abby. "Pickups have chips in them!"

For a moment, Abby couldn't follow her sister, then she realized. "If they were in the truck on the way here, then ..."

"Then it would have broken down. Everyone's would have. They could be hundreds of miles away!"

Abby felt her stomach lurch. Rae was right — there was no telling where their truck would have stopped. It was an unusually frosty late December, and even if it wasn't yet snowing where their father was, it was chillingly cold, especially for anyone on foot.

But there was nothing they could do about that. She got out of her chair and kneeled beside her sister, stroking her hair and tracing her tears as they rolled down her cheeks. "Listen, I know you're scared, so am I. But we've got to think about ourselves. What would Dad say if they got here, and we hadn't made it because we were too worried about them?"

"And Mom. She'd be angry, too."

Abby nodded. "She would. At me, probably, for letting my little sister down. And I need you."

"For what?"

"You're ten times smarter than me. And you paid a lot more attention when Dad was going on about his emergency plans."

A wet smile interrupted Rae's sobbing. "You thought he was crazy."

"Maybe you're right. But the question is — what do we do now? Dad said to stay indoors, but the generator's in the shed."

Rae wiped her nose and looked across the yard to the tin-roofed structure at the end of the grassy strip that their father called a lawn, but anyone else would say was just weeds.

"We can't be hurt by just going across there, I don't think. We're going to need power to get the TV on, or the radio. Somewhere we can get news.

"Anyway, that's where the basement is."

Abby groaned. "Of course. It was too creepy for me. Much more the sort of thing you and Dad would be interested in."

Anyone who didn't know the property would have no idea that under the log-lined shed was a cellar several times as big. It had been built when the first cabin had been put on the site fifty years before, but when their father had bought the property and ordered the original one torn down, he decided to keep the basement and build the shed on top. So, the main cabin only had a shallow space under the floor, and long-term supplies — especially those that benefitted from being kept cool — were stored in the old basement.

The generator itself was housed in the wooden shed so it could be easily accessed, with the fumes drawn through a long hose and expelled via a chimney at the edge of the property. An armored cable fed power into the main house.

"Please tell me you know how to start the generator up," Abby said.

Rae smiled, wiping her eyes. "Dad made me learn. He said there wasn't any point showing you because you weren't interested, so you wouldn't remember."

"He was right enough," Abby replied, though she felt a little jealous. Or was it sadness at her father's disappointment in her? "But I could do with a shower."

"That works off the wood burner. Don't tell me you thought the hot water was electric?"

Abby flushed. "Frankly, I hadn't given it any thought."

"But you loaded the furnace often enough!"

"I thought that was just for the heating! We're not all nerds, you know!"

Intended as an insult, all this did was make Rae giggle, her sadness disappearing, as it generally did, like a cloud after a storm. "Didn't Jesus say the geeks shall inherit the Earth?"

"This isn't a good time to be blaspheming, little sister. We might need all the celestial help we can get."

"Well, let's start by getting the generator running."

Rae leaped out of the chair and headed across the grass toward the shed. Abby followed, a little more cautiously. She didn't know what she expected to happen once they ventured out from the shelter of the cabin, but her father had been insistent.

She then had to wait outside the shed while Rae ran back to the main house for the key which hung on a bunch beside the back door.

She found the right one instantly and unlocked the padlock. The shed smelled a little of damp wood, and Rae flicked the light switch to reveal the generator beneath its tarp. "Solar panel on the roof, before you ask," she said, pointing at the light.

"I wasn't going to ask," lied Abby. "What about the panels on the cabin roof?"

"They feed a twelve-volt circuit in the house. Good for some lighting and charging up cells, but nothing that needs a lot of current. If we want the TV, we need the generator. And the fridge, of course. And the main lights so you don't fall over your towel in the bathroom when you've had your shower."

A little bit of Abby was beginning to regret that her sister's mood had flipped so completely. But only a little.

Together, they pulled the tarp away, filling the air with dust, and Rae took a ring binder from beneath it and opened it to the first page. "There's a special checklist for starting it up the first time."

Abby watched as her sister went through the list one thing at a time, beginning with a visual inspection. "Does it have gas in it?"

"Yeah. Dad makes sure the tank is full before we leave on the last day. It's got a stabilizer in it so it doesn't oxidize too much, but he thinks it's better to have gas in there than emptying it. He runs the generator with the fuel shut-off valve to make sure the carburetor is drained."

Abby smiled. "Thanks for the full explanation."

"You're welcome."

Sarcasm was lost on her sister.

When she was finally ready, she gave three pulls on the cord and the generator spluttered into life before, after a few seconds, settling down to a regular rhythm. "A little water in the gas," she said.

"Nicely done, little sis."

Rae flashed a smile, then rolled up the rug that occupied the middle of the wooden floor. Beneath was a trap door that she unlocked before pushing it back to expose the stairway heading into the basement.

She switched on the lights. "Are you coming?"

Abby looked over the edge, shivering in the cool air currents wafting up. "Remember that bit in *The Lord of the Rings* when Pippin looks into the well in Moria?"

Rae chuckled. "Don't worry, there's no balrog down here. There's probably a few spiders, but they're not Shelob's descendants. I promise, if we hear the sound of a hammer, we'll run for it and head for Lothlorien."

Taking her sister's hand, Abby gingerly made her way through the trap door and down the first steps, which creaked authentically as she went. When she reached the bottom, she looked up nervously at the rectangle of light, wishing she was up there, seized by an irrational fear that someone might appear and swing the trap door shut, burying them alive.

"Have you ever been down here?" Rae asked.

"Dad made me come down once, when I was a kid, but I screamed the place down and he never asked me again. And I don't remember it looking like this at all."

Rae made her way around a wide wooden bench and ran her hands over the surface. "It's changed a lot over the years, or so he said. I've only been here a few times. He liked to get away from us all, so he didn't invite me very often. And Mom didn't like me being down here."

Circling on her heels, Abby took in the rectangular room. It was many times bigger than the shed above and had been laid out zonally.

"That's the supplies area," Rae said, coming to stand beside her half-sister and indicating several rows of shelves, some freestanding and others screwed to the brick-lined walls.

Abby gestured at a metal cage. "Weapons? I had no idea."

"Me neither."

They wandered over and looked inside. "A couple of handguns, a shotgun and I guess that's a hunting rifle. Not enough to start a war with, but still..." Abby shook her head. Her father was the most genial, passive of men, and had never shown the slightest interest in weapons of any sort. "This is so weird. I mean, I understand about the generator — power cuts happen often enough out here — but this is like some sort of survival shelter."

Rae nodded. "Yeah, I know what you mean. But I guess he was being prepared in case we got cut off by snow or whatever. Anyway, we don't have to use any of the guns, do we?"

"No. The supplies might be useful, though."

"Here's the inventory," Rae said, taking a clipboard off a nail driven into the stair banister. "We can take that back with us, if you want, but we'd better keep it up to date or he'll kill us when he arrives."

"Let's get out of here, then."

"Sure, but first I want to take a look in Dad's office." She headed past the stairs and opened a door beneath them that Abby hadn't noticed before. Inside was a desk with bits of electronics scattered across it, all organized into piles.

Rae reached over and dragged a rugged plastic box toward her. "I wonder if he finished this?"

"What is it?"

"Well, it could just be an empty plastic box, but I'm hoping ..."

Holding her breath, she opened the lid. Then she squealed. "He did it!"

The first thing Abby noticed was the copper lining the inside of the case. A small screen that looked like a tablet was embedded in the top and the bottom housed a keyboard layout set within a fixed plastic tray that had pushbuttons set within it.

"It's a cyberdeck!"

"A what?"

"It's like a computer for the end of the world. It's low power and runs off batteries. And this copper foil is a lining to protect against EMPs. Not that they'd penetrate down here, but it means it can go anywhere."

Abby ran her fingers over the keyboard. "But won't the internet go down if the power's out?"

"Sure — if the EMP is strong enough it'd fry most internet servers. But if Dad finished the software, then this box has all of human knowledge on it, so we wouldn't need the internet. Come on, let's get it inside."

Abby wasn't going to argue about getting out of the basement. She'd been comforted to see they had some food and other supplies to see them through whatever was going on. But she was less excited by the discovery of this cyberdeck thing. It was perfectly possible that this had just been a project that tickled her father intellectually, but what if he'd built this thing because he'd seen this emergency coming?

If that were the case, what else might he know about it? And would she ever get to ask him?

12

Abby & Rae

The TV was dead. No static, no lights, nothing.

Abby moved around the cabin as she and Rae worked on an inventory of supplies. They knew what was in the basement as their father had kept that list up to date, but the cabin was almost empty because their family's habit was for each to bring specific supplies for the holidays. Abby had a trunk full of alcohol, but most of the food was brought by her father and stepmother. She'd intended to drive into the local town and stock up with junk food ahead of their arrival — the original plan having been for her to have a few days alone. Then her father had asked her to pick Rae up, and now, for all they knew, they were going to be alone for a while.

And it was so quiet. Abby had left the front door of the cabin open, her ears straining for any sign of Dad's arrival, though her rational mind was more and more convinced that wasn't going to happen any time soon.

They'd found some dead birds inside the wire-fence that surrounded the property, and she knew there would be many more lying undiscovered. They'd found crows, robins and even a hummingbird, and now Rae wouldn't go beyond the part of the yard they'd cleared out. She'd spent most of her time in the basement, sitting at their father's desk and searching through his papers and checklists as if they could explain what was happening.

"We're going to have to go into town," Rae said, emerging through the back door. She was carrying the black box containing what she'd called the cyberdeck, and she put it down on the table, before turning on her heels and heading outside again.

Abby watched her go into the basement, and was about to follow her when she reappeared, carrying a foil-wrapped box-like frame that she placed on top of the cyberdeck.

"It's a makeshift Faraday cage."

The frame was covered with silver foil on back, sides and top, but open to the front so Rae could reach in and open the plastic box containing the device.

"A what?"

"It shields against any EMP."

"I didn't realize the pulse lasted that long."

Rae shrugged. "We don't know what caused it, so we've got no idea if it's still happening or whether it could happen again. I can't risk it, but you don't like the basement, and we need to talk about this."

She reached in and pressed a button on the inside of the plastic case. A small screen on the back of the lid came on and they watched as it booted up.

"So, Dad did finish the project?"

Rae typed some commands onto the small keyboard in the bottom of the case. "I reckon he'd have kept tinkering at it, but it's already got Wikipedia on it, and that's what I was most interested in."

"I thought you said the internet was down?"

"It is. I told you, Dad downloaded Wikipedia onto the flash card. There's a Raspberry Pi in here — it's a low power computer that can be run from a cellphone charge bank, and it has no moving parts so it's tougher than your average laptop. Shut the lid on this and you can lug it anywhere."

Abby nodded as her sister spoke. "I guess I hadn't thought about how important Wikipedia would be when the end of the world happens."

"You are such a drama queen," Rae said. "All we know at the moment is that power is down across a wide area and there's been something like an EMP which has shorted out all exposed electronics. That would be bad enough, but it wouldn't be Armageddon. Humanity would recover. But we need to preserve our knowledge. And, in any case, I have to build something, and the cyberdeck will help.",

Her fingers clattered on the keyboard and Abby watched as Wikipedia appeared instantly. "We need some way to know if it's safe to go out — safe for us and any electronics. I mean, look what happened to the birds."

"Like a Geiger counter?"

Rae raised a surprised eyebrow. "Exactly like a Geiger counter. I thought Dad would have one, to be honest, but I've searched the whole basement and he didn't. So, I'm going to build one."

"You can do that?"

"Always the tone of surprise, Hermione. Yes. But we don't have everything we need here."

"Of course. What are we missing?"

"A PIN diode."

Abby sighed. "Right. Don't bother explaining. Where can we get one?"

Rae's finger jabbed at the Wikipedia page. "It says here they can be found in satellite TV systems."

"And they won't have been fried by the EMP?"

"No, diodes are pretty tough."

Abby tried to rub life into her face. "So, all we've got to do is walk into town and ask someone if they mind us ripping a diode out of their TV system?"

"Yeah, that's about it. Your car will be dead for sure. And ... well, the birds ..."

"You're thinking the same will have happened to people?" Abby said, her stomach lurching as her mind fought to deny the possible scale of the disaster. "I thought you said it might just have been an EMP?"

Rae shrugged. "It might. But something killed the birds. If people were outside looking at this aurora. Well ..."

Shaking her head, Abby walked over to the front door and looked out, feeling the chill air blowing across her face. It felt so peaceful, but she was beginning to wonder if this was the peace of the graveyard. If they went into town, they'd be able to get some news, surely? And if Rae could build this Geiger counter, that would mean they could go outside without fear of radiation.

But going into town might also be risky. If society had collapsed — and if *The Walking Dead* was any guide — then people would be focusing on looking after themselves and their families, so they probably wouldn't welcome strangers knocking on their door.

And they were two young women. Abby had seen plenty of bad behavior in her career managing d-list celebrities, but how would people — men in particular — behave in a world without the rule of law? She was an attractive blonde woman who'd been hit on ever since she'd begun to mature, and Rae, though she was a tomboy, was still beautiful in her own way. And vulnerable.

"Okay," she said, looking back as her sister continued to work away at the cyberdeck, scrawling notes on a pad. "We'll head into Oakridge tonight."

"Why not now?"

"Because we need to be able to see the sky, don't we? Until we have this radiation detector you're building, the lights in the sky are the only way we'll know, and we can only see them at night. Assuming the sky's relatively clear."

"But ..."

Abby put her hand up to silence her sister. "No arguments. We plan and pack this afternoon, and we go once it's dark. Dad would want us to take care."

"And Mom," Rae added, petulantly.

"And Mom. Now, are you going to help me shut up the basement? We need to go choose our supplies."

Rae shut down the computer and sealed the case. "Yeah. I've got what I need, and I want this below ground again, just in case. It's the most important thing we've got."

"Except each other."

Rae smiled. "Yeah."

\#

Things looked different in the dark. Obvious, huh? But Abby had driven along this road hundreds of times over the years and thought she knew it like the back of her hand. The trouble was, she couldn't see the back of her hand when the lights were out, either.

She almost gave up within the first half mile as they struggled along the forest-lined lane that linked their cabin with the highway. At intervals, they passed the dark entrances to the three or four other properties along the lane, but there was no sign of any inhabitants, not even flickering candlelight. Over the years, these cabins and ranch houses had changed hands while theirs had remained owned by Abby's father, but they'd come to know some of the families that used them in the holiday season, as well as for summer vacations. The Eisenhowers, the Schumakers and, most recently, the Chakrabartis, an Indian family whose Diwali celebrations sometimes overlapped with theirs. If anyone was at home, it would be them, but there was no more sign of them than any of the others.

"I don't like this," Rae said. She was winding up her hand-cranked flashlight to keep it going, its pitiful luminescence pulsing with the movement. "I feel like we wouldn't be able to find our way back, even though I know it's just back there."

Abby patted her on the shoulder. "I know what you mean, but we've got to do it. Once we get out from under the cover of the trees, we'll get a better view of the sky and use that to orient ourselves."

There was no sign of the pulsing lights in the thin strip above them, and Abby was hoping they'd seen the last of them. In which case, this expedition to town might as well have waited until the morning.

But they needed to be sure, and, in any case, they should at least be able to talk to whichever poor devils they woke up and get some news. Assuming they didn't get their heads blown off first.

Abby felt the breeze pick up and strained to look ahead. "Here's the highway. It should get a bit easier from here."

Looking into the sky, Rae said, "It's a pity it's not clearer. I can only see patches of sky. No sign of the aurora, though, so that's good."

Abby followed her gaze. Aside from unfriendly locals, her greatest fear was that the rainbow lights would reappear in the sky just as they reached the town, leaving them to scuttle into a bolt hole like animals. For now, despite the dark clouds scattered across the sky, there was no sign of anything ominous. Rae said the moon was due to rise later, so that would hopefully help to light their route home.

"What are you doing?" she asked as Rae dragged a fallen branch out of the black undergrowth and placed it on the curve of the intersection.

"I'm marking our turning, just in case we get confused. Turn right at the branch."

"Clever," Abby said, helping her sister to put her pack over her shoulder. "Come on, let's get moving."

Town was around ten miles from the cabin, which ought to have taken no more than four hours to walk, but Abby had underestimated just how long it would take when you couldn't clearly see more than a few feet ahead of you.

Neither of them had a working watch, but the hours seemed to creep by.

In the end, it took the appearance of faint shadows on the road ahead for them to get a time fix. "It's after one a.m.," Rae said. "That's when the moon was due to rise. My feet ache," she added.

"You're kidding me? We must have been walking for six hours!"

"So, where's the town?"

Abby looked along the road, but without much hope. They'd passed several inert trucks and cars, including a sixteen-wheeler, but they hadn't approached them, and they'd seen no movement or any other signs of life in all that time. It was as if they were the only people left on the planet.

"I can see something," Rae said, suddenly. "A light!" She grabbed her sister's hand and directed it. "There, can you see it?"

Abby cursed the vanity that had caused her to refuse a prescription for glasses. And then she saw it, "Yeah. Looks like a fire. Could be candlelight. We must be near the town. Let's follow the highway, then cut across when we're level with it."

"Oh no."

"What?"

"Look up."

Just as they'd found hope in the firelight near at hand, that hope was turned to terror as, above them, a pulsing, colorful aurora emerged from between the clouds.

"We've got to get inside," Abby said. "Come on!" She began running along the highway, her hand trailing, pulling Rae along. She could tell that her sister was looking upwards. "We don't have time for that! Run!"

The thudding of their sneakers on the highway accompanied them along the road.

"It's ... so ... beautiful," Rae was saying, spitting out the words between panted breaths.

In her panic, Abby yanked on her sister's arm, causing her to stumble and, with a yell, fall to the ground.

As Abby kneeled beside her, she looked up and the vault of the heavens was aflame. She wondered if, merely by staring at the sky, she was witnessing God's wrath and whether, if so, she would survive it.

"Run!" Abby said and led Rae off the highway toward a dark shape in the nearest field. She didn't know what it was and whether it would protect them, but there was no other target, and she knew, for a certainty, that if they stayed out under the stars, they would be dead by morning.

Then, as they got within a hundred feet of what was now revealed as a barn, the door swung open, spilling light onto the ground and revealing shapes with weapons aimed at them.

"Stay there! Don't move, or I shoot?"

It was a man's voice. Harsh and full of panic. Abby and Rae stopped, holding onto each other as they panted.

"Put yer hands up! I won't tell you again!"

"Owen, they're just two kids," a woman's voice said from within the barn.

"And who are they with? That's what I need to know."

"No one — we're alone! We want to get inside. Please help!" Abby said.

The speaker, whose silhouette had resolved into an older man in blue overalls and baseball cap with a thick checked coat, looked out into the darkness as if expecting others to appear.

"Let them in, Owen, you lummox! Ain't enough died already?"

After a moment, the shotgun lowered a little. "Get inside."

Abby guided her sister past the man and into the barn's interior.

A woman strode to meet them, arms extended. "Your poor things." One at a time, she held their heads in her hands and examined them closely. "No sign of the sickness."

"You sure you got no one with you?" the man called Owen said.

"No. It's just us. We're in a cabin along the road."

Owen grunted and, as the woman continued to check them over, the barn door creaked shut.

"I'm Rose-Marie Bartlett, but folks call me Rose. This is our farm. Come and sit down."

She led them to the center of the barn, where straw bales had been arranged in a rectangle around a central brazier which held a kettle. A young man sat there, a hunting rifle leaning against his thigh. He was enough like Owen for Abby to be sure he was related, and he shared the older man's grudging welcome.

"This here's Gray," Rose said, gesturing at the younger man. "He was on watch when the rainbow started again. We hot-tailed ourselves in here. Says it's the safest place, and he's been to college and all."

Rae said, "The barn's all metal?"

"Yeah," Gray said.

"Like a Faraday cage," Abby added, ignoring the look of rage from Rae.

Gray's eyes widened, and he looked at Abby properly for the first time.

"I'm Abby, and this is my sister, Rae. Actually, she was the one who told me about Faraday cages."

"That only protects against the EMP," Rae said. "Not all radiation."

"Hay loft's full of grain," Gray said as Rose poured hot water into the coffee pot. "I figure we're better here than in the house."

Rae nodded. "Yeah. You haven't got a Geiger counter, have you?"

"No. All we got are these." He held up a star shaped piece of plastic. "Fluorescent."

"Photoluminescent," Rae said before crying out as Abby elbowed her in the ribs.

"Sure, you're right," Gray said, apparently unflustered. "Anyway, these go bright when the radiation levels are high. Not exactly a precision instrument, but better than nothing."

Owen finally left the door and came to sit with them. "Saved our asses," he said. "Rosie always said it was worth paying for the boy's college education. Turned out she was right."

"The Freys weren't so lucky," Rose said, shaking her head.

"Buried the last of them this afternoon," Owen added.

Abby shook her head. "But it was only forty-eight hours ago!"

"More will die tonight. Most folks aren't as smart as Gray here."

As she spoke, the roof began to reverberate to the sound of falling rain.

"Have you been into town?"

Owen shook his head. "I tried. Took the truck, but no joy. The road was blocked, and I didn't like what I saw ahead. Smoke, and I could hear shooting. No sign of the cops."

"Your truck works?" Rae said. "Our car's dead."

"Then I guess yours is a bit more modern than my old LandCruiser, eh?" Owen said with a wry smile. "But anyways, I got back here and we're gonna keep ourselves to ourselves until this all blows over."

"I told you, Pa," Gray said. "This isn't going to blow over any time soon."

Rose patted him on the shoulder affectionately. "Then we'll take one day at a time. You girls are welcome to stay here, if you want."

Abby saw the surprise on Owen's face, but she shook her head anyway. "We're okay, thanks. We came into town to get some supplies and ..."

"And I need a PIN diode. I think I can build a kind of Geiger counter."

"What's a PIN diode? Do you know, Gray?"

Gray shook his head, and Abby thought she detected a trace of annoyance in his expression. He was used to being the source of all knowledge, it seemed.

"Whatever it is, there won't be any here or in Oakridge," he said.

"You can find them in satellite dish systems," Rae said.

Owen looked at her curiously. "Are you serious? You're just a little kid."

"She's the smartest person I've ever met," Abby said. "If she says she can do it, she can do it."

The older man rubbed his bearded chin for a moment, then glanced at his wife. "The Freys had a dish. Don't reckon they'll miss it."

"Good," Abby said. "If it's okay with you, we'll wait here until the lights disappear, and then you could show us where to find it."

"We'll do that alright, but on one condition — you build us one of them detectors. Seems to me, if we had one of them, we'd be able to go out when we needed without worrying if we were being fried."

Abby glanced at Rae, who nodded. "I should be able to cobble together two."

"Good. We'll go to the Freys' tomorrow and help you get what you need. I guess you need to go back to your place to build this detector?"

"Yes. All my equipment is there. But it should only take a day or two, then we'll be back with one for you."

"Oh, you don't need to worry none about that, Gray will go with you, lend you a hand."

Rae was forming the protest in her mouth when the barn entrance rocked to the sound of beating fists.

Owen leaped to his feet, grabbing his gun and beckoned Gray to follow him as he strode to the other side of the door.

"Who's there?" he called over the steady percussion of rain on the iron roof.

The door began to open.

"You stop right there! You ain't gonna get no more warnings!"

The door swung outward and there, framed against the darkness, water running down his body, arms spread wide, swayed a man who, though he was drenched to the skin, looked as though he'd just emerged from hell itself.

"Randall!" Rose gasped as the man fell on his face, his body seeming to steam as he lay in the straw.

13

Grace

Day 2: Southern Texas

Walter kept the shotgun in unsteady hands as the figure shambled toward them.

"Sweet Jesus," Grace muttered. "Is that you, Brandon?" She'd seen people who'd fallen asleep on a hot summer's day, but Brandon was lobster red and almost out of his mind with the pain.

Walter handed her the gun and walked toward his friend, though he stumbled as he held out his hands.

"No! Please. Don't touch me. You got anything for the pain? Grace?"

"Back at the house," she said. "You want to go there?"

Brandon walked on. His pants were ripped and dusty at the knees, and his limbs twitched as if in terrible pain. "Got to."

Grace and Walter shadowed him, one on each side, until she sped up to unlock the gate.

She sat Brandon on the couch in the front room and gave him the maximum dose and a glass of water.

"Got anything better to wash it down with, Walt?"

Walter fetched out the bourbon and poured two glasses, draining one and handing the other to Brandon. "What happened to you, Bran?"

The stricken man swallowed the whiskey in one and held out the glass for a refill.

"Watched the pretty lights last night from the porch with May. Figured I might never get another chance to see somethin' like that. Took some Bud with me and fell asleep. Woke up in fearful pain and ... and ..."

Bourbon escaped in bubbles and drips from the sides of his mouth as he began to sob. Grace tried to take the glass, but he didn't loosen his grip and she gave up.

"What happened, Brandon?" she whispered.

"May ... May ... she was ... lyin' there in the rocking chair." He turned his tortured face to Walter. "She was dead, Walt. Dead. Knew it as soon as I saw her. Eyes shut, but not moving an inch. What do I do?" He dropped the glass and reached out in utter desperation. "What am I gonna do? God help me!"

Grace kneeled and took his hands. "I'm so sorry, Brandon. But May has only gone where we're all about to follow. This is the Rapture, can't you see that?"

"Then why ain't we been taken up into the sky?"

"We don't know what is going to happen exactly, but we got our Lord's promise, so we gotta stay strong."

Brandon exhaled as the combination of morphine and liquor began to bite. "Went to the Johnson's first, hopin' their truck worked. No sign of them. Don't know what to ... do ..."

With that, he passed out.

"It sure was the Angels that did it, then. Poor Brandon, he's in a lot of pain," Grace said, looking down at the red-skinned man curled up on her couch. "How are you feeling?"

Walter swayed a little and put his hand to his forehead. "Not so good. Why don't you call the neighbors? I'll go and sit down for a bit."

She watched him walk slowly out of the living room, her heart pounding in panic. Would what had happened to Brandon also happen to Walter? He hadn't been out all night, that was for sure. She wondered how much exposure to heaven's wrath would be fatal. Generally, very little, she imagined.

Grace picked up her hand-written contact book which was by the black military surplus phone TA-312. They had the switchboard in their house — it was the least efficient way to go about things given that they were on the end of the row of connected houses, but Walt insisted. So, she chose a circuit and turned the crank a couple of times, listening with the heavy, old-fashioned handset to her ear. Nothing. Everyone had been told to keep the clicker turned up, so Rita and Bob had either ignored him, or they couldn't hear the phone. They might be outside, of course. Or they might ...

After cranking the clicker three more times, she gave up and tried the next number. Again, nothing. She was beginning to think the darned thing didn't work when, on the third call, someone picked up.

"Hello?"

"Rita? Is that you? Grace here."

"Hello? Is anyone there?"

Grace groaned. *Release the button, Rita!*

"Oh, I forgot," the crackly voice said. "Over."

"Thank heavens. This is Grace. How y'all doin' down there? Over."

"Grace? It's so good to hear from you. Things are okay here. Oh. Over."

"Did you go outside last night? Over."

"Frank's on duty in Twisted Pine. Came back and told me about the lights in the sky. Figured he'd been drinking, so I looked for myself. I thought they must have come from heaven. But I was frightened, so I stay indoors. Frank had to go back. Over."

Grace sighed with relief. "That sure is good to hear. I got Brandon here and he's pretty sick. Walter's not too great, neither. But listen to me, I got nothing from the McFadden's, or the Gormans. I'm going to try the Levines and the Goldsteins. Then, if the sky's clear tonight, I'm going to check on them all. We've prepared for this, and I know a lot of you folks thought Walt and I were crackpots, well now we don't look so darned foolish, do we? So, I'll call you later and start walking, and I'll meet up with you. Sound like a plan? Over."

"You think this really is the end times, Grace? Over."

"Sure seems that way to me. For now, all we can do is look after ourselves. So, keep yourself safe, and we'll see you tonight. Over and out."

She put the handset down, checking (as Walter had instructed) that it was properly seated, and the call was therefore cut off.

Well, at least one of their neighbors had survived. She wasn't counting poor Brandon, because he wouldn't see the night out if she were any judge.

"Hey, Walt!" she called, striding through the house, then catching sight of him on the other side of the inner compound fence. "I got ahold of Rita. She's okay. What are you doing?"

She stood, hands on hips, as a cool zephyr peppered her lips with dust. Walter was waist deep in a hole. He stopped, put the shovel to one side and wiped his forehead. "Bran's not gonna last long. I reckon when he wakes up he's gonna wish he was asleep again. Look, Gracie, we can't spare the morphine and he ain't gonna survive, anyway."

"You're gonna kill him? On the Day of Judgement?"

Walter shook his head. "Seems like a mercy to me. Wouldn't let a dog suffer life that, much less a fine man like Brandon. It's what a friend would do, you understand? If you really care about someone, you gotta do what's right, even if it's hard, and even if it ain't exactly scriptural."

She opened her mouth wide, then shut it again. Walter was not generally a subtle man, but she couldn't help decoding what he was saying. She swung around and headed back toward the house. "No way, Walter Boone. No way."

#

The rest of the day passed slowly. Brandon remained on the couch, tossing and turning as consciousness came and went. Grace was dreading the moment he woke up properly. She could only imagine the pain he would be in. It was as if he was in Hell already, and it chilled her soul. She said a silent prayer for him, for Walter and her, and for Lyle, their good for nothing son. When the end came, she wanted him to be here. Blood was thicker than water.

Walter spent most of the day hunched over the short-wave radio searching for any broadcasts that might give them a sense of what was going on. None of the commercial radio stations were operating, and the Emergency Alert System was nothing but static. Grace could tell that this was what freaked out Walter the most. Even if the world had gone to hell in a handbasket, the emergency transmitter should still be working.

"Why don't you come and rest?" she said, poking her head around the door to the room that housed their communications equipment after several hours had passed.

She expected him to argue, but he just ran his forearm over his brow and got slowly to his feet. He stumbled, slamming his hands down on the desk to steady himself. "Leave me be, woman!" he snarled, his breath coming in short pants. He straightened himself as she recoiled, then, as he passed her heading for the door, his hand reached out and, for a moment, she felt his fingers wrap around hers. And that, of all the things she'd seen so far, froze her heart. Walter Boone was not an affectionate man, and she almost withdrew her arm in shock, but she managed to master herself and squeeze his hand. He half looked at her, nodded, and left the room.

Neither of them wanted to sit in the front room with the delirious Brandon, so they took their accustomed chairs on the porch, looking toward the road beyond the wire fencing.

"Didn't you hear nothin' on the radio?"

"What? Oh, yeah. A few others like us. Don't know anythin'. Lights in the sky yesterday, cars busted and folks gettin' sick and droppin' dead all over today. Gracie, you ain't fixin' on goin' anywhere tonight, are you?"

"Sure I am. I told you, I said we'd go check on the neighbors, then meet Rita and Frank."

"Do it tomorrow. I don't think I'm gonna be able to walk far. Not until I've rested up a little."

She put her hand on his arm noticing how he shuddered as she touched his skin. "But if the neighbors need help, they ain't gonna be able to wait. I didn't want to leave it until nightfall, but I want to know the sky's clear before I go. You rest up here, Walt. I'll go on my own."

"No, Grace," he said, leaning back in his rocking chair, breathing heavily through his open mouth. "Please."

She almost burst into tears as he said that word. Walter Boone was polite enough to friends and neighbors, but he always said that "please" and "thank you" weren't needed between husband and wife.

Taking his hand, she squeezed it and they sat together, the boards creaking as their chairs rocked, each fearing that this might be the last time they'd ever do it.

"Sure is quiet," he said, eventually, releasing her fingers. "Don't reckon I've seen a single truck go by."

"You said they're likely fried, like ours."

"Older trucks might be okay. No electronics to fry. Maybe there ain't no one around to drive them. We should go look for one. When I'm better."

She wiped a tear from the corner of her eye.

"Sure, we will."

"Fetch me some more meds, Grace, will you?"

"It's too soon."

He shook his head. "I don't care, none. I'm just awful sore."

"You want to go up to bed? Might be more comfortable there."

"Yeah. You go check on Bran, will you?"

"Can you manage up the stairs?"

He grunted as he got to his feet."

"Sure I can. Done it a thousand times."

But she noticed he just stood there, gripping the back of the chair until she'd left the room. She wanted to help, but she knew he needed to do this himself. One more victory over gravity.

When she reached the front room, she found Brandon staring up at her, eyes wide and teeth clenched. "Stop ... stop the ... pain ... G ... Grace. Please."

She looked at the pack of meds on the closet behind him. Walt had been right; they didn't have near enough pain medication. They'd assumed they might need it for the occasional injury, not swallowing pills every couple of hours.

She kneeled in front of him, her head level with his. "What do you want me to do, Bran?"

"Take it ... away ... now!"

"I'm so sorry," she said, not daring to touch him though she desperately wanted to. "I can't make you better. I don't think no one can. If I give you morphine, it'll only help for a little while."

"Give ... me a ... gun."

She nodded. "Can you walk?"

He nodded. "A ... little ... way."

Step by step, she led him out of the bedroom before leaving him to make his slow way through to the kitchen while she went to the basement and took the Ruger from the cabinet. By the time she caught up with him, he was outside, shivering as he looked into the trench Walter had dug earlier.

Tears ran down his face as she stood beside him.

"I ... guess ... I understand."

"You don't have to do anything, Brandon. If you want, I'll nurse you." She knew this was all kinds of wrong when it came to the practicalities — not least of having to look after two sick men at the same time.

But it was the right thing to do — one soul to another.

"Can you take the pain away?"

"I don't think so, not with meds."

"I ain't gonna get better, am I? I'm fallin' apart." He lifted his hand, bringing it close to his eyes and rotating the wrist to reveal a vivid ulcer.

Again, she reached out to touch his shoulder, but stopped herself. She looked down at his hand, and she gently took it.

"You got the gun?" he asked.

"Sure."

He nodded, then sat down on the edge of the trench before allowing himself to fall, howling with pain as his legs scraped against the rough, stony sides.

Then he turned, and reached up, taking the gun from her outstretched, shaking fingers.

"Leave me be, now. Grace."

And so, she left him there.

She was just halfway up the stairs when she heard the sound of a gun firing.

Walter had obviously also heard it. "Poor fella. He was a good man. Did it hisself?"

"Yeah. I sure hope the Lord lets him into Heaven anyways. How are you feelin' now?"

"Ready for some meds. And don't argue none, Grace. Just leave them by the bed."

Grace crossed her arms. "I will not. You need 'em, I'll give 'em to you, but I ain't giving you the whole bottle."

He sighed and held out his hand as she counted out the pills.

Minutes later he was asleep. She watched until the tension left his body, and he was finally peaceful, the only sound being a regular half-snore that told her he was unconscious. She breathed a sigh of relief and made her way downstairs, taking the blanket she'd put over Brandon and walking round to the grave. He was lying on his side, the revolver a few inches from his mouth. The shadows of late afternoon mercifully covered any more evidence of his violent end. She wasn't about to clamber into the grave and retrieve the gun, even though she knew Walter would do it if he were here. Fact was, he wasn't here, and she was not about to leave poor Brandon out here without burying him first. So, she said a short prayer over him, then heaved the first spadeful of gritty soil on top of him. She covered him enough for decency, then, blowing with the effort, she turned away, with a final Amen and, as she did so, she felt the first drops of falling rain like tears from Heaven.

14

Elijah

Day 3: Glendale, CA.

He could see daylight peeping between the drapes when he finally woke up again. Tentatively, he moved his head, lifting it slightly, and finding that the headache had receded.

"Oh, you're awake," she said. "Would you like some ramen?"

"What time is it?"

"About nine. You've been asleep since you got back with Cody. I'd offer to make you some oatmeal, but I'll only mess it up."

"Noodles would be great, thank you. Any noise from upstairs?"

She shook her head. "What happened at the pharmacy? You didn't say nothing."

"I was exhausted, Becky. To be honest, I don't remember everything. I'd passed a pharmacy on the way here, so we went back, and I covered Cody while he found what he needed. Took a while — the place had been turned upside down."

"No one bothered you?"

Wade shrugged. "A couple tried, but I wasn't in the mood to be nice. I think they noticed. But we've done what we can for Cody and his sister."

"How long will the meds last?"

"I don't know. They'll have to work out the minimum dose they can get away with."

"And what then?"

"Jeez, Becky, I don't know!" he snapped. "I've done my best for them, but I can't take responsibility for everyone!"

Her face froze, and he felt shame overwhelming him. "I'm sorry. I want to be able to help, you understand? But there's only so much I can do. Now, I've got to get to the hospital."

She relaxed, then walked into the little kitchen. "You need to see someone, fosho. But then there must be plenty like you, who got sick from the radiation."

"It's not for me. My partner, Terry, he should be there. He was sick. Real sick. Then I need to head back to the station."

He heard the click-click of the gas lighter.

"I'll come with you," she called. "You need looking after."

"Have you been outside today?"

"No. Someone came to the door. Said she was a neighbor and asked where 'nice Mr. Lynch' was."

"What did you tell her?"

"I said he'd asked me to look after the place. I don't think she believed me. But her husband was sick, she said, and she wanted his help."

She returned and handed him the plastic tub of ramen.

"Thanks. Are you okay? Your hand's shaking," he said, before gasping. "Oh my God, I'm sorry. My brain's still scrambled." The poor young woman had been kept in a locked room, tied hand and foot, until he'd rescued her. And then he'd collapsed, and she'd been left alone in the middle of chaos. He'd woken up, then they'd gotten involved with Cody and Shelley. He wondered whether, in fact, she'd stuck with him because she couldn't bear to be alone.

"It's okay," she said, rubbing her ankles. "I guess I knew you needed me, but right now I feel like I'm holding back a flood, and if I think for too long, I won't be able to stop it."

Wade put a forkful of ramen in his mouth. It was undercooked, but he swallowed it and put the rest of the pot down to soak up more water. "Do you want me to take you back to your apartment?"

"Apartment? I thought you knew all about me."

He sighed. Of course, he'd researched her once she'd gone missing in circumstances that bore the hallmark of a serial killer. She'd been living in a shared room owned by a notorious pimp who'd briefly been a suspect in the abductions.

"Do you honestly think Luigi would take me back now, even if whatever this is hadn't happened?" She gestured at the world beyond Lynch's apartment. "D'you think I'd want to go back even if he did? He doesn't care about me. I was only any use to him because of my looks, and now I'm damaged goods."

"Your parents live in Florida, is that right?"

She nodded. "Yeah. I came out here to become a movie actress. I was just a kid. Got swallowed up by the Hollywood system."

"Yeah, I've heard your story plenty of times. Why didn't you go back home when you realized it wasn't going to happen?"

She shrugged. "I had my own reasons. But, anyway, I haven't got anywhere to go, so I'll stick with you."

"You will?"

"You rescued me, so I'm your responsibility now. Otherwise, what was the point?"

He finished his ramen and regarded her. Mid-twenties with jet black hair and a slim figure, dried tears marking out a prematurely lined face. Like a thousand others. But, unlike Becky, the others weren't his problem.

"I won't abandon you," he said, as he perceived her desperation. "That's a promise."

It was a promise he knew she needed to hear, but he felt the weight of responsibility settling on his shoulders as he said it.

"You mean that? You just said you didn't want to be responsible for Cody and Shelley."

"Yeah. I didn't get a dose of radiation running across the city to rescue you, and then leave you to fend for yourself."

He got to his feet, steadying himself against the wall for a moment before making his way back into the bathroom. The water was still running, so he soaked a towel and used it to clean himself as best he could, feeling life and alertness returning as he did so. His guess was that the lights caused some form of radiation sickness or, perhaps, that they were a signal of some other cause. Either way, he'd gotten enough of a dose to make him sick, but hopefully not enough to kill him.

He was certainly feeling better than he had when he'd first woken up, but he had no time to rest up any longer. Once it was dark, and he could check the sky, he had to go to the hospital and check on Terry first, then head to the station. One way or another, he needed to get a handle on what was going on here and elsewhere. And he had to work out a way to get in touch with Kelly. He didn't want to think about what was happening two thousand miles away.

A couple of hours later, they were ready to venture out. He gave his Colt 1911 Bureau model a quick check. "Ready? We won't be coming back."

She held up the knife she'd taken from the kitchen and nodded.

"Remember, keep behind me and let me handle any trouble, okay?"

He thought she was going to snap back, but she merely said, "Okay. Let's go. How far is the hospital?"

"Not far."

He opened the door a crack, holding the weapon close and peering into the night. It was quiet — unnaturally quiet. He'd always lived in the city, and the background noises of car horns, music and people shouting at each other had become the canvas on which his life was painted. Now, it was as if someone had whitewashed normality and the silence pressed down on him as he edged out, scanning the dark between shadows for attackers.

"Clear," he said, then glanced up at the sky. He could see stars, but no rainbow lights. Breathing a sigh of relief, he moved silently toward the road, eyes straining to make anything out in the darkness.

As the echoes of Becky's footsteps faded away, he listened again, looking back and forth along the road, the horizon illuminated by the glow of fires raging downtown. Now he could hear voices calling far off, but there was no sound of moving vehicles. From time to time, the crack of gunfire sounded, seeming to come from random directions. The deeper thump of, perhaps, gas cannisters suggested either that the police or national guard were trying to impose control, or that the mob had gotten hold of police equipment.

"I've changed my mind," Wade said as they sheltered by the side of a store, shards of glass scattered across the pavement and reflecting the orange glow. "I'm going to report to my district station, then check the hospital later. You sure you want to come?"

"Nowhere else to go," Becky said. "I guess I'll be safer there than most places."

Wade grunted an acknowledgement, then led her across the street, retracing the route he'd taken to get to Lynch's apartment.

"Where is everyone?" Becky asked as they paused to catch their breath.

Wade shook his head. "Hiding in their homes, I guess." He'd been pondering this as they'd run through the dying city. He'd seen plenty of looters when he'd been going the other way, but it was as if that madness had burned itself out and been replaced by terror. He imagined families cowering behind barricaded doors, praying that the government would rescue them before their food ran out or the mob took over completely.

Or maybe they were sick. Or dead. As far as he could tell, he hadn't been exposed to the radiation for more than a few minutes — or, at least, not directly. How many tens of thousands had looked up at the sky in awe and wonder, not knowing that they were receiving a lethal dose?

"Can I ask you something?"

"Sure."

"Why don't you just head out of the city? Everything's gone to hell here. What's the point in going back to the police?"

"I'm a cop, it's what I do."

"You're also a father."

"Lucky for you I didn't head off before rescuing you," he snapped, unable to hide his anger. She was poking at a sore, much more painful and dangerous than the one on his neck.

"I'm just saying ... Look, this is the end, you know what I mean? I haven't got anyone who gives a damn about me. You got your daughter. If you were my dad, I'd be waiting for you to come get me."

He glared at her, struggling to hold back his anger at her insight. She was right, of course. He was a father first, a cop second. But Kelly was thousands of miles away across a country on fire, whereas his police family was right here, within reach.

"Look," he said, forcing himself to be calm. "I can't just run away. I've got friends here, friends and colleagues, and I need to do what I can to help them before I go."

It felt ridiculous to even consider attempting a journey across the continent. Was he going to walk the entire way? He'd ridden horses from time to time, but he was no expert, and it was a long way even on four feet. And all of that was aside from the fact that he'd be traveling across a hostile land, a sitting duck for any bandits that wanted to take what little he had and leave him with nothing more than a bullet in the head.

No, he could make a difference here. Perhaps.

But Kelly needed him. If she was still alive.

So, he would attempt the journey. But first he would do all he could to help save his city.

15

Hannah

Mauna Kea

Hannah watched as the man finished the third energy bar and tossed the empty wrapper in the trash. The Grach pistol lay to one side, just within reach.

"Is okay. I will not shoot you. Here." He took the gun and ejected the magazine onto the table. "I use it only for protection."

"Who the hell are you?" Shane said. He was standing some way away, looking out into the darkness as if others might suddenly appear.

"My name is Lev Makarov and I was part of Kozlov team."

Hannah couldn't help being curious. "Hunting exoplanets?"

"*Da,*" he said, before waving his hand. "But I am not scientist. Sorry, I am not *a* scientist. My English is not good, but I try to learn."

"You don't look like an administrator," Shane said.

Makarov chuckled. "No. I am, what you would call? Fixer? Security?"

"Why would you need that?" Hannah asked as he finished the last energy bar. "This is Hawaii."

"Hawaii, United States of America. Many nosy parkers. We mind our business. All gone now," he made a noise like an explosion, his hands spreading wide.

In the dim emergency lights, Hannah could see Shane gesturing outside. "Kozlov's a couple of miles that way, isn't it?"

"*Da*."

"How many survived?"

Makarov pointed at himself. "Many died here, I see. All dead at DSST. I walked to find someone alive."

The Deep Sky Survey Telescope was the nearest observatory to theirs and lay between them and Kozlov which was in a cluster of smaller facilities near the summit.

"Why did you come?" Shane asked, not bothering to hide his Aussie bluntness.

Shrugging, Makarov said, "It is better to be with living than dead, no? Perhaps I can be useful."

"How?"

"Digging graves? I help."

"And what do you want in return?"

The Russian got to his feet. "Just to stick around for now. You will see, I can help. Here, have gun. But if we go out, one of us must be armed."

"Why?"

"World has gone to hell. We must look out for demons."

Shane strode over to Hannah and tugged her arm, leading her over to the door.

"Sure," Lev called, "decide if you want my help. If not, I go. But no monkey business."

Shane leaned in. "What do you think?"

"I think we need help digging the graves."

"Then what?"

"Jeez, Shane, I don't have any long-term plans. Maybe a holiday on the Canary Islands?" she said, before taking a deep breath. "He can help us bury our friends. When he's done that, we owe him somewhere to sleep. Tomorrow, we can decide what happens next."

"Do you trust him?"

"I barely trust you."

His face screwed up and she wished she hadn't said it.

"I'm sorry. I'm edgy, that's all."

"Look, it's okay," he said. "But, for the record, you can trust me."

She hugged him, forcing herself not to recoil from his sweat-laden aroma. She guessed she probably smelled much the same, after all. Then she waved Lev over. "Let's go."

"Oh cool, I am in grave-digging club," he said, tucking his weapon into his pocket and gesturing around. "Where do we start?"

Even with three of them working together, Hannah was beyond exhausted by the time they pushed the trolley up the slope for the final time. Behind them, in the pre-dawn light, a dozen mounds protruded from the ground, each bearing a pebble with the name of the grave's occupant written in permanent black ink. Around two hundred and fifty years of scientific experience and wisdom left to desiccate in the volcanic dust.

#

Day 3

It was after midday by the time Hannah awoke, Kuchinsky's mechanical clock one of the few reliable timepieces left working. She could hear Shane showering in the next pod along, and she sighed with relief at the prospect of getting herself properly clean. But she wanted to check on their visitor first, so she climbed out of bed, put on her soiled clothes and made her way down to the ground floor.

Lev emerged from the basement stairs as she gazed around, double checking for any bodies they might have forgotten in their exhaustion. Getting those who'd died in the shipping containers up the steps Lev was now climbing had been the hardest task of the night, and she was grateful time and again that they'd accepted the Russian's help. He'd volunteered to sleep down there when they'd gotten back, claiming he didn't have the energy to climb to the upper floors, but Hannah had locked the door on her pod in any case.

"*Dobroye utro*," he said. "Though I think no morning is good anymore. But look, I did not murder you in your sleep. It is morning and I am still here. See, I am good Russian. You are English and Shane, he is Australian, is he not? Sounds like joke: 'English, Australian and Russian go into bar.'"

In the daylight, Hannah saw an entirely different man. Short and lean, Makarov had a blunt, open face that wasn't remotely handsome, but somehow managed to be appealing. She guessed he was in his late thirties or early forties, but his boyish looks reminded her of a peasant in a cheap fantasy film.

"You have not eaten? I get some food together while you have shower."

"It's okay," Hannah said, suddenly aware of how hungry she was.

Lev shook his head. "No, is not okay."

She felt herself redden, then turned and climbed up the stairs, passing Shane on his way down.

"Don't take long," he said. "We need to have a council of war."

By the time she returned to the cafe area on the ground floor, she found that Shane and Lev had piled up the chairs and pushed the empty tables against the windows. She was glad. This way, she wasn't being constantly reminded of the missing.

The observatory was reasonably well stocked with pastries sealed in plastic wrappers, along with preserves, and they tucked into them with abandon. Soon enough, the fresh milk would spoil, and the bread products go stale. Then they'd be left with canned and dried foods but, just for today, they could eat as much as they wanted.

"So, tell me," Hannah said as Lev folded a final pastry into his mouth — a mouth that seemed too big for his face, "what happened at Kozlov? I guess everyone went out and looked at the lights like here?"

Lev looked apologetic. "Ah. I thought we would have to talk about this."

Shane choked, then spat out fragments of part masticated toast. "You son of a b—"

"Is okay! I told truth. I was only survivor."

"So, what is there to talk about?"

Shrugging, Lev took in a deep breath. "I was only survivor because team had all gone. Took commercial flight."

"The whole team? When was this?" Hannah was amazed — observatories were expensive to maintain and were generally busy with science work every possible minute.

"It was a week ago."

"And they left you alone? What did they say?"

He nodded. "I was like caretaker. They had data. Could not be trusted to upload. I think ... I think ..."

"What is it?" Hannah asked, leaning forward.

"I think they knew. I think they knew about lights. And they left me to die."

"What?" Shane said, his mouth dropping open. It would have been funny, except Hannah was just as shocked.

"Let me get this clear, in case something's being lost in translation. Are you saying they knew that this radiation storm — for lack of a better word — was coming?"

Lev shrugged. "I think so. Many arguments, but they did not tell me. Then they left and told me to guard observatory. Told me not to go out if lights in sky."

Shane slammed the table-top, then got up and walked back and forth, obviously unsure what to do with himself.

"My God, they could have saved billions of lives," Hannah said.

"I think, perhaps, they tried. But they were not free to speak — our government is not like Western governments."

Shane stood over Lev, hands on hips. "They're scientists, aren't they? They could have brought their data to us!"

"No, they could not. They are scientists, you say? *Da. Russian* scientists. They do not consult, or share without permission, and they would not dare to trust communication systems within United States territory."

"So, they decided to travel themselves and present their data personally? Is that it, Lev?"

The little man shook his head. "I think so, maybe. I am not scientist. But I am Russian, and think like Russian. They have families. I have family."

"Wait a minute," Shane said. "Maybe they *did* get their message through. He sat down opposite Hannah. "Don't you see? Maybe this disaster only happened here? Maybe everyone else hid out of sight? Our families could be okay?"

Hannah felt hope rise for the first time since people had started dying. She didn't want to believe it was possible, any more than she'd wanted to accept that billions of people might have died. "We need to go to Kozlov. Take a look at their data."

"I do not think it is there," Lev said, shaking his head.

Hannah looked at Shane who was staring through the glass in the direction of the Russian observatory. "I wouldn't be so sure. They told you to secure the facility and not to go out when the lights were in the sky?"

"*Da.*"

"Then, as a scientist, it's inconceivable that they would have wiped their data entirely and gotten on a plane with the only copy. If that's the case, why leave you behind? What were you protecting? No, I reckon the data's still there."

"It'll be in Russian," Shane said.

Hannah reached out and put her hand on Lev's. "Will you help us?"

He paused for a moment and then shook his head. "I was given orders. Authorities do not give medals to men who think for themselves."

"Lev, the world might have ended, billions could be dead. Who cares about politics?"

"Then I agree," he said, abruptly. "If world finished, then I help you. If not, then no."

Shane sighed, leaning back in his chair. "And how are we supposed to find out?"

"You are scientists, no?"

So, they agreed a plan. Lev and Shane would secure the observatory and create an inventory of their supplies — including gas for the generator and the state and capacity of the solar panels. Hannah would go to the control room and look for radio signals and other indications that the world had survived the apocalypse. She had bitten back her hope that the Russians had alerted the world. After all, if they hadn't heard, here at a vital node of the electronic scientific community, then what hope was there for people who were more remote? The best-case scenario: hundreds of millions had died.

And, while she was working in the control room, she also needed to find a way to monitor radiation levels, otherwise they wouldn't know when it was safe to make the trip to the Russian observatory. The aurora might have been a one-off, but she wasn't going to bet on that, especially after what Bixby had said. How tragic would it be for humanity to survive the first blow only to be finished off by not watching for a follow-up punch.

She reached the control-room where she'd last seen Kuchinsky alive, hunched over his computer. Avoiding his station, she sat down at the site supervisor's position and, after searching for a while, found and flipped the power switch at her feet.

She was rewarded by a sound of whirring, but the monitor array remained dark and the activity lights on the computer bases remained invisible. She kicked the table. Of course, this room was right at the top of the observatory. Perfectly shielded from any normal amounts of radiation, but if the fate of her friends and colleagues was any guide, they weren't talking about normal anything.

She checked all the computers, but none booted up. The only other computers were the scientists' laptops. She thought of hers — it was on the bed in her container room — would it have survived the EMP? Good grief, if the radiation had penetrated that far, then they had no hope at all. So, she made her way downstairs, back to the catacombs beneath the observatory.

It was weird being down there again. The corridor made by the line of container bedrooms on one side and the pair being used as the storage area on the other had been a familiar place of laughter and fun until just a few days ago. Now it echoed to nothing but her footsteps and the occasional sounds of Shane and Lev moving in the food cellar.

Hers was the bedroom next to Shane's, and she listened to the familiar squeak of the hinges as tears ran down her eyes. For the first time, she'd stopped for long enough to think about what had happened, and her mind was now trying to gently begin the process of understanding: the first step to coming to terms with it all.

This uncertainty was the most frustrating thing about the situation. But surely the word would have gotten out? How, though? The aurora took out communications, it seemed, so the people dying beneath it would have no way to tell anyone still in the Earth's shadow that it was happening. She clung onto hope that whatever the planet had moved through had dissipated before the last of the surface was exposed to it.

She picked the laptop up from the bed — the bedclothes exactly as they'd been when she'd last kicked them off, back when things were still normal — gathered up some fresh clothes and toiletries, then made her way back up the first flight of stairs and back to the bright light of the observatory.

Returning to the control room, she plugged the laptop into the data feed interface for the small radio telescope that sat some distance from the observatory. Designed for detecting signals from unimaginable distances, she wanted to listen for a closer signal, for the voice of Earth.

But that was going to be tough. She could get the raw signal into the laptop, but the instrument had been designed to filter out humanity's noise. It was like looking down the wrong end of a telescope.

Like most astrophysicists, she was a pretty adept programmer, especially when it came to creating algorithms, but this was work that would normally have taken days, even if it could be achieved at all. She rubbed her eyes as footsteps approached from behind and a steaming cup of coffee was put on the desk beside her.

"There you go, Han. I reckoned you'd probably be ready for a hot one."

She smiled at him and waited for the inevitable question.

"Me and Lev have finished the inventory. We're okay for a few days, I reckon. For food and water, at least. Fuel's going to be more of a problem. The solar panels are working, but they're only any good for low power stuff."

She slapped him on the arm. "That's it! You're a genius!"

"I am?"

"Let me think!" she said, waving for him to leave her alone.

Low power. That was the answer. She cut the current to the radio telescope, so it became little more than a passive antenna. Deaf to the sounds of the universe, but perfectly capable of picking up Earth-derived transmissions.

There it was. A signal. One, clear signal on a single frequency.

She ran to the balcony that looked down on the lower two levels and called to the others. "I've got something!"

Her hands shook as she sat tapping on her knees waiting for them to join her.

Shane was the first to arrive, followed by the slower footsteps of Lev who emerged from the doorway surrounded by a cloud of cigarette smoke. "Sorry. Was taking break."

"I've isolated a digital radio frequency that's broadcasting."

"Ah, that is good! What does it say?"

"That's what we're about to find out. The radio telescope feed has a demodulator. It was only put there for fun, really, just so we could hear a representation of the radio waves we received. The sound of a black hole, for example. But it also works for regular radio transmissions. Here goes."

She clicked a button on her laptop and turned the volume up.

A familiar voice filled the control room, but she knew instantly that it was a recording.

"...of the United States, broadcasting on the Emergency Alert System. My fellow Americans. An unimaginable catastrophe has befallen our nation, and the world as a whole. We have experienced levels of radiation never seen before. We do not believe that this is the action of an enemy as its source appears to be from space. And all nations have been affected.

I am sorry to tell you that hundreds of millions of our citizens have died and that many more will follow them. Please be assured that we will restore government as soon as possible and provide relief and support for the survivors.

In the meantime, I have one crucial message. Do not go out if the aurora is in the sky. This means, do not go out in the daytime, or if the night sky is cloudy.

Stay hidden, stay underground as far as possible, and look out for each other.

And may God help us in our hour of greatest need.

God bless you all. And God Bless America."

They stood in silence as the message repeated, and then Hannah switched it off.

"Well, I guess we have answer," Lev said. "And now, I will help you. We must know if this will come again. Tomorrow, we must go outside."

16

Abby & Rae

Abby poured the hot water from the kettle into a bowl and carried it across the barn to where Rose kneeled beside the wreckage of a man.

Owen wandered around, nervously scratching his scalp, as if worried he might catch something. Gray stood by the door looking out at the falling rain, rifle slung over his shoulder. Rae was hiding in the shadows somewhere.

As Rose dabbed his wounds, the man groaned.

"What in God's name were you doing out, Randall?"

The man had a badge on his chest and wore a deputy's uniform. "Been ... out ... all ... day. Sheriff ... aah!"

He winced and Rose withdrew her hand. "I'm so sorry. I wish I could take the pain away."

"Liquor?" the deputy croaked.

Owen got up and brought a bottle of bourbon across which he held at the man's tortured lips as he drank desperately. "Hey, go a little easy. No tellin' when we'll be gettin' any more."

"Owen!" Rose hissed.

The older man stood up and walked over to where Gray stood, looking out on the night.

Abby followed him and, to her surprise, Rae appeared out of the darkness behind Gray.

"Seems to me it's a waste of good whiskey," Owen said, speaking to his son.

"Seriously?" Abby snapped. "That's what you're concerned about?"

Gray jabbed a finger at her. "Don't you go talkin' to Pa like that. You haven't had to do what we've done today. You weren't up at the Freys' place when we found them."

"They're radiation burns, aren't they?" Rae said.

Owen shrugged. "I guess so."

"And the Freys looked the same?"

"Yeah. Irving, Mary and their two kids."

Abby saw something pass between Owen and his son, something in the way they looked at each other. She joined the dots. "They weren't all dead, were they?"

The older man glanced over at where his wife was tending to the deputy. "She don't know, I didn't tell her. The young'uns were both gone when we got there. Mary was near the same, and Irving looked a lot like Randall there. We watched as she died. Hours it took. Hours of pain and nothin' we could do to help. When she'd gone, he begged ... begged me."

Water drained into the wrinkles around Owen's eyes, though Abby had to look twice to be sure she was seeing it.

"I knew it was wrong, God knows it. Do not kill. That's what the commandment says."

To Abby's astonishment, Rae looped her hand under Owen's elbow and leaned her hand on his shoulder. "Didn't Jesus say 'Do unto others as you would have them do unto you'?"

Owen looked down on her and patted her short hair. "You're right. And I sure wouldn't want to go through his pain. Or Randall's."

"But Randall isn't asking," Abby said.

Gray looked back into the darkness. "He will. Soon enough."

\#

Day 3

Abby didn't see it happen. They had to wait until the lights had faded, so Rose could be sent back to the house while Owen and Gray remained in the barn talking to the now delirious deputy.

A shot rang out, amplified, it seemed, by the iron roof and walls of the barn. They were half way to the house, and Rose stopped for a moment at the sound, but then continued walking. She knew what her husband intended and would, in time, be grateful that he hadn't involved her in the terrible decision or the action itself. Owen had said that Gray would wait outside, and, when it was done, he'd help his father deal with Randall's body.

Rose led them wordlessly into the farmhouse, boots echoing on the wooden boards that made up the platform the house stood on. Rae held the photoluminescent star which glowed feebly as they went inside. The sun was still below the horizon, but there was enough light, even on this cloudy day, to make their way through the dark house.

"Here," Rose said, at last, "we can sit in here." When she lit a candle, Abby could see that they were in a sitting room with a couch, too easy chairs and a brick-built hearth. "Owen says we can't have the fire on unless the drapes are shut, but we can't hide forever." She thrust the curtains apart, then busied herself at the log fire. Within minutes, a living flame was crackling away, and she fell into one of the fireside chairs, wiping her eyes.

"Sweet Jesus, I've known Randall since he was a boy. His wife lives in the town. Owen had better go tell the girl."

Abby, who'd sat next to Rae on the couch, said, "I'm so sorry. I hadn't imagined it would be this bad."

"That could have been Dad," Rae said. "That's what I keep thinking."

Abby put her arm around her sister's shoulders. "There's no point. Dad's super smart," she said in a low voice.

After a few minutes of silence, heavy footsteps could be heard on the steps outside. "That's Owen," Rose said. "I need to tend to him."

"What can we do to help?" Abby asked.

Rose turned as she got up from her chair and headed for the door. "Just don't judge him. Things have changed, probably forever, and the old rules don't apply."

Settling back into the sofa, Abby looked out through the white-framed window at the slowly growing light.

"That man wouldn't have died if he'd had a detector," Rae said.

Abby ran her fingers through her sister's short hair. "We don't know how he came to be outside, but you're right. We've got to get a detector working. I'm not happy about Gray coming back with us, though."

"He seems like a nice enough boy ... man," Rae said.

"I don't want anyone to know where we live. Our best chance is to stay hidden until ..."

"Until what? This isn't going to blow over, you know?"

"I don't know what's going to happen. For now, we have to take every day as it comes, and it's safer if we can hide out in the woods."

Rae sat up and looked at Abby. "I don't think they're going to let us walk back home with the diodes without Gray. We've just got to trust him and hope he's okay."

Abby settled her gaze on the crackling, roaring log fire. As a creature of the city, she'd only ever experienced a real fire when on their vacations to the cabin, but she'd never really and truly looked into the flames and understood the raw power of the elements. As civilization collapsed, the survivors would find themselves much closer to nature than they might want to be. This was no wild-camping trek, this was the renewal of the deep connection between humanity and the elements without the protective blanket of mankind's inventions that, for thousands of years, had kept the natural universe at arm's length. As she watched the flames dance, she imagined the uncounted generations of humans that had done the same thing and she wondered whether her generation would be the last.

\#

It was late morning by the time they were ready to go. Abby and Rae had both helped dig Randall's grave at the bottom of the field, on the edge of the property. There were only two shovels, so their participation had lengthened the time it took to finish, though its symbolic importance was undeniable. Owen would carry the burden of what he'd done, but not the additional weight of their condemnation.

Rose made each of them a sandwich — with the last of their bread — and watched as they headed away from the farmhouse and up into the tree line. A pine wood marked the northern border of the Bartlett farm, and the overnight rain meant that, as they walked, they released a scent that reminded Abby of disinfectant.

Every now and again, Gray would pause beneath a tree and examine the little fluorescent star but, so far, he'd seen no sign that the lights were behind the clouds, invisibly irradiating them.

They stopped after an hour to eat — Owen told them they probably wouldn't have much of an appetite once they got to the Frey's farm. "It was a cattle farm," he said, by way of explanation. "Nothin' we could do about them. Didn't have enough bullets for them all."

Owen wore a detached expression. She'd seen the same sort of look on drug users, though she doubted Owen was a user. He was like a robot, going through the motions. She resolved to get away from the Bartletts as soon as she could.

She nudged Rae as they trudged along. "Maybe we should make a break for it and head toward the town."

"Why? We know those poor people from the farm had a satellite system, so I should be able to find what I need."

Abby slowed her pace a little, so they fell back. "Don't tell me you're not freaked out a bit by them?" She gestured at the two men,

"Not really. They've both been through a lot ..."

"Enough to make most people crack."

Rae glanced at her. "Look, you're much better at this sort of thing than me. Understanding people, I mean. But have you got any clue where we are right now? Could we make it back to the road without them catching us, even if we wanted to?"

Truth was, they both knew they stood little chance, and, in Owen's current state, Abby wasn't going to trust him not to shoot as she ran for it. "Just keep an eye on them, okay? We get what we need and then go."

"With Gray?"

"I'm still hoping to find a way to avoid that. Are you sure you can't make the device without going back to the cabin?"

"I didn't bring the cyberdeck with me. That's got the circuit diagram on it."

Abby grunted.

"Here we are," Owen said as they emerged from the pines and looked down on a scene of horrifying contrasts.

At first, it was the silence she noticed, then she saw what had, at first, seemed to be small brown and black mounds, gathered in groups on the dusty yellow soil below. As her eyes adjusted, she noticed the tiny shapes tearing at the mounds, then flying away.

"Not a big ranch. They had around five hundred head," Owen Bartlett said. All dead. Damn shame. Come on, we'll follow the line of the trees. Direct route to the farmhouse is across there, and I guess none of us wants to go that way."

Abby grabbed Rae's hand as she heard her sister sobbing quietly beside her. "Come on. Let's get what we need and get out of here. Where's the satellite going to be?"

Gray said, "Generally attached to the house. But we don't want to go inside unless we have to."

"Why?" Rae asked, wiping her tears away.

Gray looked directly into Abby's eyes as if unsure how to answer.

"Let's just do what Gray says," Abby whispered as she held Rae close. "How far is it from here?" She directed this question to him.

"About a half hour."

Abby nodded and guided Rae along. She patted her pocket to reassure herself that she had her sister's meds there. This would not be a good time for an attack. She'd have come on this journey alone if she could have done, but she knew nothing about technology and her chances of identifying the right part were close to zero.

So, she kept her gaze on the grassy bank they were walking along, and the trees to their right, and tried not to look at the horror on their left.

There was no way to entirely avoid the stench of death as, even when they'd spotted the ranch, they still had to walk between open paddocks where shapes lay where they'd dropped. Abby couldn't imagine how many crows and other carrion birds had been killed by the radiation, but she was grateful that the air wasn't full of their delighted cawing. How had any survived? Come to think of it, how come neither she nor Rae had shown any symptoms at all? Sure, they'd been inside the cabin, but it wasn't entirely made of iron like the Bartlett's barn, and she couldn't work out how it was that so little radiation had penetrated the roof to leave them apparently unaffected. Perhaps, for those who weren't outside under the lights, they'd become sick, but later. She remembered watching *Chernobyl* on HBO — most of them had only found out they'd been fatally exposed days later.

Maybe this was all futile. Even if they found a satellite setup, *if* Rae was able to find and extract the part she needed, *if* she was able to build a radiation detector — it could all go perfectly, and they'd only then discover they'd received a killing dose.

"I'm going to have to get up there," Rae said, snapping Abby out of her dark thoughts.

"Go fetch a ladder, son," Owen said, then watched as Gray ran off to the nearest barn. "You got everything you need?" he added to Rae.

"I think so."

"You're not going up there!" Abby said. "You don't like heights."

Gray arrived with a rusty ladder that he leaned against the wall.

"Can't Gray do it?"

"He doesn't know what he's looking for."

Owen gestured up at the dish, which was fixed beneath the apex of the roof. "Gray can get the case off, then all you got to do is find what you're looking for."

Abby had a sinking feeling in her stomach. This was already an utter nightmare. But this was likely to be their one and only chance. In a few days, this place would stink beyond endurance, and she had no desire to ever return.

Gray took a small roll of tools from his backpack and then clambered up the ladder, before immediately beginning work on the casing.

A few minutes later, the first panel of the rusty box that protected the electronics fell with a clattered to the ground.

Soon enough, it was Rae's turn. She took much longer than Gray to get up there, and Abby positioned herself immediately under the ladder as if she could catch her sister if she fell off.

"I can't do this!" Rae said, when she was only halfway up.

Abby shielded her eyes against the bright, cloudy, sky. "Do you want me to come up with you?"

"Ladder might not take you both," Owen said.

"You'll have to do it on your own," Abby said. "Think of it like a game. Go for a high score."

"Like Minecraft?"

"Yeah."

"No one plays Minecraft anymore."

Despite her fear, Abby sighed, but Rae was moving again.

And then the wind got up and rattled the ladder. Rae screamed and grabbed the rusty rungs.

"Come down!" Abby called. "I've got an idea."

"I ... I can't move!"

Abby jabbed a finger at shape clinging desperately to the ladder above. "Rae Waterman! Now you get your butt down here right now, or you're grounded!"

Rae went still, then looked down at Abby. Then she started moving down, rung by rung, until Abby reached up and grabbed her.

She hugged her sister momentarily, then took the black canvas tool bag off her, rummaging through it. She found the biggest, flat-bladed screwdriver, then clambered up the ladder, forcing herself to keep looking straight ahead, and to ignore the wind whistling around her. When she got to the top, she braced herself against the now exposed innards of the satellite system.

"What are you doing?" Owen called from below.

Abby ignored him. She found the screws that fixed the rusty box to the wall, then reached over and pushed the tip of the screwdriver into the gap. She gritted her teeth as she pulled on the handle, now regretting her bravado. Why hadn't she asked Gray or Owen to do this? Because she hadn't wanted to feel useless? *Nicely done, Abby. Nicely done indeed.*

Then, as she was about to give up, the metal groaned and the wall plug emerged, bringing the first screw with it.

"Are you crazy?" Owen called.

"Get out of the way," Abby yelled back. "This baby's going down."

But this baby put up a lot of resistance. She decided to work on the remaining two screws alternately, hoping that the unit would then drop from the wall once they'd come out so far.

And it was working. The second screw was half out, and she was levering the third one. Any moment now, it would drop, and they could get out of this place of death.

Then, quite suddenly, the third screw popped out and all the force she was using to lever the metal frame off the wall was pushing against thin air.

The frame fell.

So did Abby. She flailed at nothing as the ladder swung back, the sky went by in a blur. She felt the impact. And saw nothing more.

\#

"Abby? Abby! Wake up!"

At first, she could see nothing. Rae's voice seemed to be calling from far off, as if Abby had fallen down a well.

Then she saw a circle of light. *Had* she really fallen down a well? Was that the opening?

No. It was getting bigger. Her vision was returning.

"Don't move," a voice said.

"Dad?"

"Sorry, kid. No. It's just Owen. You took a hell of a fall. But you got to come round slow, like. Now, can you move your fingers and toes?"

She'd never had to think about moving them, but now it seemed as though she had to remember where they were, her mind moving along pathways that had almost been severed. Like a computer that's been restarted.

"I see them!" Rae said, the relief in her voice obvious.

"Yeah, that's good. Now why don't you go tend to Gray while I see to your sister?"

The silhouette of Owen's face appeared above Abby. "Does anything hurt?"

"Everything hurts."

"I mean, like, broken hurt?"

She went to shake her head and winced.

"I said keep as still as you can. If you're real lucky, you only jarred your neck, but it's gonna be mighty painful."

"I remember, now."

"That's good."

"I fell off the ladder."

"You did."

"I thought I was going to die."

"Well, you would have done if Gray hadn't caught you."

"What?"

Owen looked at something nearby. "When I say he caught you, well, he tried, sure enough. But you came down on him like a sack of bricks and I think you might've cracked a rib, maybe worse. Jeez, how we gonna get you both home?"

17

Abby & Rae

Rae followed Owen as he moved a little away from where Abby and Gray lay, side by side. She could still feel the adrenaline coursing through her body from that moment when her sister had fallen. She'd thought Abby was dead, and the minutes she lay there unconscious as Owen checked on his son were the longest of her short life.

She didn't blame the older man for concentrating on Gray first, and only then turning his attention to Abby, but it was a reality check for her. Family came first. Especially after the end of the world. And the only family she could be certain of was lying on the cold concrete.

In truth, Rae hadn't liked Abby that much. Her tall, blonde, capable half-sister was everything she wasn't. She got to work with movie stars — going to parties and premieres and film sets — while Rae spent her time with textbooks and teachers and fellow students who were two years older than her and full of resentment. They called her Sheldon.

But when her sister had fallen, she'd realized how much she needed her. And, perhaps, that was what love was, when you got down to it.

"You got any ideas?" Owen was saying. "You're the smart one, by all accounts. Even Gray says so."

Rae looked from his face — all crags and hair and sandpaper skin — to the figures lying on the ground. "I'm not a medical doctor."

"Sure. But it don't take a genius to know that we need to find shelter for them. Now, Gray we can move. It's gonna hurt, sure enough, but he's a tough kid. Your sister, well, like I said, she needs shelter, or she'll die of exposure or shock. But I'm worried about her neck."

"Where would we go?"

Owen looked past her. "We got no choice. Into the house."

"But you said we couldn't go in there."

"Beggars can't be choosers, kid. You and me, we'll have to clear out the living room, bring a couple mattresses down and tend to them there. At least we'll be able to get warm."

"Then what?"

"Then we work out how we're gonna get home. Now, d'you reckon it's safe to move your sister?"

Rae looked over at Abby and realized her sister was looking back at her. "We'll have to carry her on something and immobilize her neck."

Owen scratched his chin. "I'll find somethin' to put her on, you wrap her up nice and tight."

The older man disappeared while Rae thought about how she was going to protect Abby's neck.

"What's in there?" she said to Gray, who was now propped up a little and watching her.

He shrugged, then grimaced. "Don't know. Animal ... pen. Wouldn't go in there if I was you."

Which, of course, made Rae's mind up for her.

"Where are you going?" Abby said.

"Looking for something to bind up your neck."

Abby tried to reach up to her as she passed by. "Gray ... said ..."

Rae ignored her sister. She was at a loss, and she didn't want to go into the house without Owen. She pulled on the rust-edged metal door, the screeching of the hinges causing a fluttering of wings as crows took to the air.

She paused for a moment, tentatively sniffing the air for the stench of death. Good grief, a couple of days before, she'd had no idea what that smelled like. This was a new world, and she didn't like it one little bit.

It was a kind of workshop. The far wall was lined with tools, and a long bench took up most of the space beneath that. Hanging up behind the door was a sweater. She took it down and used a pair of shears to cut it into strips, then returned to where Abby lay and bound them around her neck.

"I'm sorry," Rae said as her sister squealed with pain. "I've got to do this."

She turned at the sound of footsteps to see Owen dragging a single mattress out of the ranch's front door.

"Best I can do," he said. "I've cleaned out what I can from in there, but I don't advise going upstairs."

They shimmied Abby onto the mattress, and she lay there rigid, her neck wrapped up tight, grimacing as Rae and Owen pulled the mattress in through the front door and then into the living room, that looked out onto the main courtyard.

Then they returned and helped Gray to limp into the house, one arm over each of their shoulders.

Finally, they were inside, and Owen slammed the door against the cold wind. "I'll set a fire," he said, and began piling logs from the basket beside the hearth.

"Pa, that'll give us away," Gray said. He'd been propped up on the couch, his face pale and pain in his eyes.

"Give us away to who? There ain't a whole lot of point stayin' secret if we freeze to death in the meantime."

Rae kneeled beside Owen as he worked. "Why don't you want anyone to know we're here?"

The older man didn't look at her, but, instead, took a lighter from his pocket and plunged it into the paper and kindling beneath the log pile. "Folks do all kinds of crazy things when they're scared. And when they reckon no one's around to stop them. You weren't the first folks to turn up at our place."

That made sense. Owen had looked alarmed when they'd arrived the previous day.

"We sent them on their way with their tails between their legs. Reckon they went looking for easier prey. But they could still be around, and they may not be so easy to scare next time."

Rae left him to it and went to sit with Abby. "How are you?"

"My head hurts like hell. And my neck. But I'm alive."

Abby looked up at Gray. "Thanks, by the way."

"You're welcome. You could do with losing a few pounds," he said. "Might not have cracked my ribs, then."

"Funny," Abby said.

Rae looked daggers at Gray, then settled down and stroked her sister's hair. "Don't listen to him."

"It's alright," Abby said. "He's not the first man to tell me I have to lose weight. God help me, I used to pay attention to them, too."

"Hold on a minute, I was only joking," Gray said."

Rae wagged a finger at him. "Then you've got a crappy sense of humor."

"It's okay," Abby said. "Gray saved my life. That buys him a whole stack of credits."

Owen got up from the fire, which was now blazing away, warm air filling the small living room.

Rae said, "Can I go upstairs and see if they've got any meds?"

"I'll go. What are we looking for? Advil?"

They watched him head out, then his big boots could be heard on the ceiling before he returned. "Got a little here. Better split it between them."

He handed the meds over and Rae gave some to Abby first, then Gray.

"It's getting dark," Owen said, sitting in the armchair. "I'm goin' back to the farm. Fetch the truck round. Should've brought it in the first place, but I ain't sure when

I'll be able to get any more gas for it. You kids sit tight. I'll be back in the morning."

He got to his feet, shook his son's hand, and, after a final glance at Abby and Rae, left, shutting the door behind him.

"He's very brave," Rae said, suddenly feeling alone. "I wouldn't like walking that way in the dark."

"He's done it hundreds of times," Gray said. "His boots would find their way even if he couldn't see a darned thing."

#

But, come morning, Owen hadn't returned. Rae woke up in the cold light to find that the fire had died down. Abby was asleep under her coat, though they'd all had a disturbed night made more difficult by her need to go to the bathroom. The bucket was outside the back door. Rae shook her head, amazed at what she could do for her sister when it came down to it.

Gray had gotten up first, and claimed to be doing a perimeter check, though Rae suspected he was concentrating on the track that led into the center of the farm.

Abby stirred, and Rae kneeled beside her.

"How are you?"

Abby rubbed the back of her neck. "Sore."

"You're shivering."

"I'm okay."

Rae got up and looked around the living room for anything she could use to cover her sister. Nothing. She'd have to venture into the parts of the house Owen had warned her against. In truth, she was curious about what she might find behind the door in the corner of the room. But it was the kind of horrific curiosity that drew people to public executions, the type of compulsion that told a dark tale of the heart of man.

She got up and, casting a glance out of the living room window but seeing no sign of Gray, she opened the door. It led onto a hallway with a flight of stairs, dimly lit as if the drapes were closed throughout the house. And there was a smell here. Not the rank miasma the wind had brought their way as they'd crossed the fields of dead animals, but nevertheless, an undercurrent of fear and despair.

She didn't want to go on; at least, that's what she told herself. The stairs creaked as she made her way upstairs, gripping the handrail, but keeping her eyes fixed on the landing in case something lurked there, ready to ambush her.

The bathroom door was opposite her when she reached the top, and she could see where Owen had been searching for the Advil, boxes of pills littering the floor, and, no doubt, continuing inside beyond the reach of the weak light.

Three other doors led off the landing and she took the handle of the first. It had to be a bedroom, and she'd surely find a comforter here for Abby. She shivered as the back of her neck bristled with goosebumps.

"Don't be an idiot," she hissed under her breath. "Owen and Gray buried the bodies, even if they died in here."

She opened the door, saw the ghosts of two single beds, and felt her way over to the shut drapes. She thrust them apart and then looked around.

She saw the beds. She saw the bloodstained comforters. And she saw the bullet holes in the wall.

She ran from that place, onto the landing and down the stairs.

Into the arms of Gray.

She flung herself backward, but his hands gripped her arms, and she couldn't move.

He looked down at her, his jaw clenching and releasing, but whether from the pain in his ribs or anger, she couldn't tell.

"Pa told you not to go upstairs, didn't he?"

"He ... you ..."

"I came back to tell you I'm going to check on him, bring the car round. Maybe he's had trouble with it. Maybe he's had a different kind of trouble. You can stay here and wait with your sister."

Rae shook her head. "But you ..."

"Don't you say nothing you're gonna regret, Rae. Your choice whether you wait for me here or try to make your way on foot. Your choice whether you reckon you owe us anything for saying your asses."

Then he swung around and, without another look, went out the open front door.

#

After another couple of Advil, Abby was able to sit up and tentatively look around, testing her range of movement.

"You shouldn't be moving it at all," Rae said.

"No, you're right, we have to get out of here, though I'm not sure how far I can walk just yet."

Rae gave her sister the last quarter of yesterday's sandwich and got up. "I'm going to look around. See if there's a truck or something I can get started."

"Don't go far. And don't be long."

Rae smiled and headed out the kitchen door into the main courtyard. Past the barns, she could see a row of piled up earth that must be the graves of the family who'd lived here. She wondered if they'd all gone out on the night of the lights and marveled at the sky, not knowing they were receiving a fatal dose as they did so. And she wondered what the bullet holes meant.

Gray had taken his glowing star with him, so she had no idea what the radiation levels were at the moment. But she felt like she had no choice but to try to find some way out for them. She didn't trust Gray or his father since she'd been in that bedroom. Maybe there was an innocent explanation, but it sure looked as though someone had shot them as they lay in bed. Owen hadn't mentioned finding them that way. And, given what he'd done to the deputy, maybe he'd seen it as a mercy, but it had a frenzied look about it that didn't suggest it was a calm, rational act.

Of course, there was every chance that Gray would be back at some point that day, but Rae wanted to be ready if he didn't return. She'd snipped the diode out of the satellite system, but she couldn't build the radiation detector here so, without any other way of knowing if they were being radiated than by looking up into the night sky, they'd have to wait until it was dark. Assuming she could find some transport.

She thought she'd struck lucky, but then saw that the truck's windows had been smashed in. Puncture holes in the doors suggested it had suffered the same fate as the people upstairs. It was a recent model, in any case, so it probably wouldn't have started. She was looking for something older.

And, in the end, she found it. A tractor sheltered under a small iron roof on one side of a cattle field. She picked her way past the bloated carcasses, thanking the creator that a light, frosty snow had locked in the scent of death. This place would have been a hell on Earth by now if the lights had appeared in the middle of summer.

The tractor — a John Deere in rusty-speckled green — had a trailer on the back with sacks of cattle food. Rae, who'd never gotten up close to a tractor, climbed up, then found the ignition. Good, the key was in it. Less good, the transmission looked like a medieval torture device. It looked as though it had eight forward gears and three reverse. Well, she wasn't going to need to go backward, but, for now, she didn't want it to go forward either. She just wanted to know whether it would start. It was a cold morning, and this was an ancient diesel tractor. She pushed the lever to the P marking, then held her breath as she turned the key.

The engine turned over, spluttering but not catching. Rae knew next to nothing about engines, but her only option was to try again. It was on the third attempt that it roared into life, like a machine gun going off. She shut it back down immediately and looked around from her vantage point on the seat as the echoes died away. Nothing moved, at least not yet.

She got down and hurried back to the living room, where she found Abby standing on her feet, her hand at the back of her neck.

"What was that? It sounded like someone shooting."

"I found a working tractor," Rae said. "If they're not back by nightfall, and there are no lights in the sky, we're going to have to risk it."

"To get home? But we'd go straight past their farm! They'd hear us!"

"All I know is, we have to get away. We can head into town and find a back lane. Try and cut across to the cabin."

"How do you know how to drive a tractor? Oh, you don't, do you?"

Rae collapsed into the couch, pulling her coat around her shoulders. All her feelings of triumph had disappeared under her sister's questioning. And, of course, Abby was right.

On the other hand, she didn't want to just sit and wait for Gray or Owen, or both, to come back. She had a bad feeling. Their farm would only be a few minutes away by car, and she could only think of bad reasons for them not returning.

"I think we should go now."

"What?"

"It'll be dark in a couple of hours, but maybe we can get back to the cabin by then."

"What about the radiation? How can we tell if we're being exposed without seeing the sky?"

Rae slid her butt over the front of the sofa until she was sitting on the mattress next to her sister. For the first time, she wondered how it was that there was no blood on this one. "Look, something horrible happened upstairs, and I think Owen — and maybe Gray — did it. We have to get away. I'll keep us under cover as much as I can, but we can't stay here, don't you understand that?"

Abby looked at her sister as if trying to divine her state of mind. Then she nodded. "Right. I believe you. Now, help me up."

Rae took both of their packs as she led Abby across the field to where the tractor sat beneath its rusting iron roof. She could hear Abby moaning as she kept the wrapping tight around her neck to give it some minimal support. This was going to be awful for her. At best they'd get the tractor moving and she'd lay in a trailer with no suspension, every second agony.

But she didn't complain, and Rae found her admiration for her sister rising. She'd always considered Abby something of a pampered princess, but she knew that was largely the selective thoughts of a jealous sibling. There was no place for such shallowness at the end of the world.

The end of the world? It was odd. It was so quiet. And it had, it seemed, happened overnight when she was asleep.

What was that poem?

This is the way the world endsThis is the way the world endsThis is the way the world endsNot with a bang but a whimper.

Yes, that was it. T.S. Eliot. She'd expected firestorms, riots and gunfire. Maybe those things were happening elsewhere, but here it was a field full of dead animals and other silent witnesses of Armageddon. It was as if a switch had been flicked. And yet she was still alive.

Time to make some noise.

She helped Abby into the trailer, impressed that her sister didn't complain about the filth as she crammed herself into the middle of the sacks of grain, though Abby saw the tears running down her cheeks.

"We'll be home soon," she said. "I promise. Have you got your gun?"

"Yeah. But I can't guarantee I'll be able to react quickly."

"You'd better let me have it, then," Rae said.

Abby looked into her eyes. "Sure."

"What? You mean it? You said I'm just a kid."

Abby shrugged. "I trust you. It's easy to use. Press the safety, aim and fire. Jeez, I hope you don't need it."

"Me too," Rae said, taking the gun, surprised at how heavy it was. She felt a surge of love for her sister, and pride, too. And fear. Things really were bad.

She climbed up into the seat and thought about her mom and dad. She imagined them making their way on foot over the miles between wherever their truck had stopped working and the cabin. What would Dad say? Something encouraging, she was certain. She doubted that he'd ever driven a tractor, but he would tell her to take it slowly, one step at a time and observe the effects of her actions as she took them. And he'd tell her, above all, to make sure she kept herself and her sister safe for when he made it to them.

She looked out from the seat. The sky was full of gray clouds and a cold, gentle drizzle had begun to fall. Maybe that would reduce any radiation exposure? She cursed herself for persuading Abby to go on this expedition with her for the sake of the diode. They should just have waited at the cabin for Dad and Mom to arrive.

But no point crying over spilled milk. She worked out a course that would take them around the lifeless humps and toward the road. She turned the key and the tractor grumbled into life again. She'd worked out that the machine must have independent brakes with one pedal on either side, and that the transmission would determine the speed, but that was all. The rest was going to be pure experimentation.

"Here goes," she said under her breath. Rae grunted as she moved the selector, which seemed to group the gears in pairs. She chose first gear and the tractor lurched forward as she grabbed the wheel.

They were moving at a snail's pace, but that was good because it gave her a chance to get used to the steering. She practiced with each of the brake pedals, noting how much pressure was needed to take effect.

Then, once they'd cleared the shelter and she could hear the rain pattering on the open cabin's roof, she shifted into second and carefully steered her course, keeping her eyes away from the still shapes.

Growing in confidence, she shifted up again, but something ground inside the engine, then she realized she had to move the selector to the side and then down and back to the left to move between groups of gears.

So, she bypassed one pair and chose fifth, the wind and rain refreshing on her cheeks as the tractor crawled toward the ranch.

"You okay?" she called over her shoulder.

After a moment, she heard Abby call, "Yeah. Well done, sis!"

She was actually enjoying this. Even here, in the midst of disaster, a frosty breeze blowing, rain falling on her and, for all she knew, being exposed to deadly radiation, she laughed into the wind.

This was cool!

She swung the tractor onto the lane that led to the main road. When she got to the end, she would turn to the left, head toward town and then find a route to the north, heading roughly in the direction of the cabin.

Then she saw something lying in the road. Too wide for her to steer around. She could run it over, as it was obviously dead. Or, she'd have to move it.

She brought the tractor to a halt and put it into park.

"What are you doing?" Abby called.

"There's something in the road, I'm going to move it."

She ignored Abby's protest as she climbed down, and jogged over, wiping the rain from her eyes. Her hope that it was just a coat that had blown across the road disappeared as she got nearer and she pulled the gun out of her pocket, pressing the safety.

Then she recognized who it was. "Gray!"

She held the weapon out in front of her, two handed like she'd seen in the movies. He didn't move when she poked him in the back, and she wondered what had happened to him.

He was lying on the wet ground, face pressing against the dirt and the collar of his coat flung upwards as if he'd been blown off his feet.

She pushed on his shoulder until he rolled on his back. His right arm, which had been hidden under him, was covered in a red stain that polluted the muddy water beneath.

"What is it?"

Rae started at the voice, then turned to see Abby there. "It's Gray. I think he's ... he's dead."

Abby lumbered past her and bent down to grab his boots. "Come on, let's get him out of the way."

But, as she pulled, Gray groaned.

"Oh, my God. What do we do?"

Rae knew what the *human* thing to do was, but she desperately wanted to get back home. And, in any case, they were supposed to be escaping from Gray. But then, he'd been shot by persons unknown.

"Come on, we'd better get him in the trailer," Abby said.

"Are you serious?"

Abby shrugged. "He saved my life. I may not like it much, but it's payback time."

"But we'll have to take him back to the cabin! What if he shot those people? We can't trust him. Can we?"

"Maybe not. But we've got to try. He probably won't live, but it shouldn't be because of us, should it, Rae?"

Rae got up and impulsively pulled her sister into a wet embrace, then reached up to kiss her on the cheek.

Abby whispered, "We got this, Rae."

18

Samuel & Ruth

Day 3: Pennsylvania

Samuel drove the cart back to the cluster of English houses and jumped down as he saw Ruth walking toward him. He patted the flank of the gray mare he'd liberated from the Millers' stables. She'd been working hard ever since, moving supplies that had been gathered by the foraging parties into the garages of this newly forming community.

A surge of love threatened to overwhelm him as he held his wife, her coffee skin lined with care and exhaustion.

"Thank the Lord you're safe, Samuel."

"How are things here?" He'd been away for half the day and had fretted the entire time, pondering endlessly on the meaning of it all, and praying that his wife would be there waiting when he returned.

She stepped back, shaking her head and wiping her face with the back of her arm. "We lost two more this morning. Oh, Samuel, it doesn't seem as though I can anything to help them. Victoria says we should help those who are beyond saving."

"What does she mean?" Samuel began unloading, nodding at a young man with blond hair to come help.

"They're in such pain, she wishes to ease their passing."

"To kill them?"

"They're going to die anyway."

"We're all going to die. It's for God to decide when that is to be, not Man. Here, Justin, these are medical supplies, you know where they go?"

"I do, Mr. Gerber."

"Thank you,"

Sam watched as the young man moved away, then turned his attention back to his wife. "I'm sorry, I know it's not as simple as that. But I don't want you involved in, you know ... Let them do it, if they must."

"Of course. Did you have success with your foraging?"

"Some. Ethan and Thomas have been remarkably efficient at scouting out the supplies we need." The two men had volunteered to go into the nearby town and gather supplies, leaving them out for Sam's cart. Well, the Millers' cart — but they weren't going to need it again in this life. He'd spent most of the past thirty-six hours bringing the most useful supplies from their barn to feed the survivors, few that they were. There was no reason for anyone to starve. It was medicine and fuel that bothered him the most. The weather was worsening, and so the next job would be to go from house to house and find any propane cylinders they could use to keep this small cluster warm. All the survivors had been gathered into four ranch houses, and that might turn out to be one too many to keep warm.

He thought of his own home. If he were there now, the fires in the living room and kitchen would keep the whole house warm, but this wasn't the way of modern times. Gas furnaces were much more efficient, to be sure. Until the gas stopped flowing, and the electricity that powered the pumps. They'd rounded up enough generators to keep the lights on, but that was about all they could achieve, and they rotated a handful of electric heaters among the rooms to try to keep the sick warm.

There were three fit women: Ruth, Victoria and Maisy Proctor, and a couple of older women who hadn't been struck down by the dancing lights, but who could do little more than sit with the sick and watch over them.

Aside from Justin, who was, even now, returning to take another box of supplies from Sam, the only other men in the community were Ethan and Thomas. Ethan was, like

Justin, in his late teens, but cut from different cloth entirely. Where Justin was a good, well-behaved and respectful young man, Ethan was more typical of his generation. But Thomas, who was in his forties, had taken Ethan under his wing and put his restless energy to use in the foraging party.

So, these seven were entrusted with the care of over twenty sick people — and they'd begun with closer to thirty.

Sam caught Justin as he finished unloading. "I guess we've got digging to do."

\#

Samuel was thinking about sleep when he spotted something moving along the road. They'd chosen to dig the graves on a small rise overlooking the ranch houses that sheltered the survivors, and he'd fallen into an exhausted rhythm as he flung the heavy, wet soil out of the trench. From here, he could see the roofs of the town's nearer dwellings, separated by no more than half a mile of highway. Plumes of smoke had risen from many of them, so he knew that some people, at least, were sheltering there. But around him lay signs of ruin — the field pockmarked by fallen birds and both domestic and wild animals. He'd been forced to throw the body of a fox into a nearby hedge because he couldn't bear the crazy, tortured expression in its face as it stared sightlessly at him.

"What's that, Mr. Gerber?"

So, Justin had also seen it. A flatbed truck headed along the road from the town. Though he didn't have good eyes — even with glasses on — Sam thought he could see people standing in the bed. He hoped it was just his imagination, but Justin confirmed the worst.

"Maybe six or seven in the back, some of them with rifles. What are we going to do?"

"Get ourselves back to the houses. Maybe they'll pass us by, but I want to be on hand in case they don't."

Sam began running down the hill. He didn't need to have seen Mad Max to know that this looked bad. What would happen when civilization fell, as it surely had? The violent would rule. At least for a time. He had no idea what God's plan might be but, for right now, he needed to be near Ruth.

He reached the bottom of the hill just as the truck stopped outside the house. A man in a wide-brimmed hat got out of the front seat, took in the scene and opened his leather coat to reveal a gray uniform beneath with a gold badge.

"Afternoon, folks. Name's Sheriff Strickland. Who's in charge here?"

All the women turned to Ruth, who had come outside with Maisy Proctor, who pushed the children behind her. Ruth looked across at Sam. "My husband, Samuel Gerber."

The newcomer raised his eyebrows. "You Amish?"

"Mennonite."

"Ha! Thought that was a kind'a fossil."

Sam didn't respond. He already knew what sort of man he was dealing with. The kind who derived his authority from pushing others down. Not unique to English, but certainly more common.

Strickland — if that was his real name — waited for a reply that never came. His eyes shifted around, and he glanced over his shoulder as if to check his gang was behind him. And it was a gang, that was obvious enough. Five men and one woman, most in denim jeans, all obviously armed.

"Where are your deputies, Sheriff?" Sam asked.

McCullock's eyes narrowed. "Somethin' wrong with your eyesight, son?" He gestured behind him. "Sure, they're in plain clothes. Helps us blend in and keep order. Now, you gonna invite me in, or not?"

Sam looked across at Ruth, and then at Victoria. Both women shrugged. They all knew they had little choice.

"We're caring for a lot of sick people," Sam said. "We're not geared up for hospitality."

"Oh, that's okay. My boys will stay out here, and you can fill me in on how things are goin'."

"I can tell you that without going inside."

Strickland shook his head. "Well, all the same, I wouldn't mind a sit down and a coffee if you've got such a thing."

Maisy stepped forward and pointed to the door of the house on the end of the group — the house that had been hers. "Sure, Sheriff."

She led the way, as the man smirked at his followers. Sam whispered to Justin, "Will you keep an eye on things out here? Fetch me if you need me." The boy nodded, nervously, and Sam patted him on the shoulder.

He walked with Ruth into Maisy Proctor's house, his mind going back to when he'd first come in here to chaperone Ruth as she tended to Maisy's husband. A man whose grave lay among the others on the rise above the house. He remembered how strange it had been to be inside an English house, but also how utterly trivial that seemed to him now.

Behind him, he heard the footsteps of the children running into their bedrooms, giggling.

The adults went into the kitchen, which was being used to prepare meals for the community, and Ruth helped Maisy move equipment and ingredients off the table so they could sit down.

Maisy poured warm coffee into a mug and slid it over to Strickland, then offered one to Sam.

"No, thank you."

"Looks like you've got yerself organized," Strickland said, taking off his hat to reveal greasy white, thinning hair, and putting it on his lap.

"It's been hard," Maisy said. "We've got so many people to try and care for."

"Do any of them survive?"

Maisy shook her head. "Not so far, but they were the sickest. I hope we'll save some."

"What do you do with them's who won't make it? It's not so hard to tell, is it?"

Ruth's mouth opened wide. "We care for them. We just said so."

"You give them food?"

"Of course."

"Folks who are dyin' anyway? Not very smart when supplies are short."

Sam tapped on the table, struggling to cover up his anger. "It might not be smart, Sheriff, but it's the right thing to do. Everyone deserves loving care."

"Maybe the best thing to do would be to put them out of their misery. You ever thought of that?"

Ruth and Maisy exchanged glances.

"Yeah, I thought so. You know, this is why this new world needs leaders. The kind who'll make the tough call."

"Leaders like you?" Sam said.

Strickland spread his arms wide, smiling, and held up the sheriff's hat. "Well, if the cap fits."

The corridor reverberated to the sounds of running feet and Justin appeared in the kitchen. "Mr. Gerber! They're taking our supplies!"

"What?"

"I suggest you sit back down," Strickland said, drawing a revolver from the holster under his jacket. "My boys are redistributing, that's all."

"But we need those supplies!"

"Well, think of it as a kind of re-education. You're now gonna have to prioritize who you feed, who you tend, and who you don't. Just say the word and my boys will help, if you can't do it yourself."

Sam saw Maisy moving behind Strickland, but he gave the tiniest shake of the head, and she froze.

The sheriff looked over his shoulder. "Of course, you Amish are pacifists." He spat the last word like a curse before pointing at Maisy, "Now, just you mind yerself. Too many have died already, and all we want is a contribution. And you stay where I can see you," he added to Justin, who was standing beside Sam.

Then they heard gunshots, and Strickland spun around. "What the hell?"

In that moment, Maisy grabbed a knife from the kitchen drawer and leaped across the room to plunge it into Strickland's back. The crack and thud of gunfire outside was overwhelmed by his yell of pain and fury. He threw her off and, in a smooth and practiced motion, fired two shots into Maisy's chest.

"Mommy!"

Kaitlin ran in, and Strickland's gun came around, but Sam threw himself forward and grabbed it, the shot going up and out, the window exploding in shattering glass.

Ruth was on her knees, cradling Maisy as Kaitlin and Logan sobbed beside their mother. Justin pulled the knife from Strickland's back, causing the man to convulse, screaming in agony, and then the blade swept down, and the so-called sheriff went still.

Justin took the gun from the dead man's hand and brought it around as boots thudded toward the kitchen.

"No!" Sam called out, grabbing Justin's hand as he pulled the trigger, sending the shot into the ceiling, a shower of plaster raining down on them.

Ethan emerged, gun sweeping the kitchen, before kneeling beside Maisy.

The bloodied face of Thomas followed him inside where he stood, trembling. "Jeez, not Maisy," he said. "At least you got him."

He pointed down at the still form of Strickland.

"Where are the others?" Sam asked.

"Three dead, two run off. We got a hell of a mess to clear up out front."

Justin embraced Thomas. "Thank God you came back when you did."

"That weren't entirely by chance. We saw their truck when we were scavenging. Nearly got caught by them. We knew they'd come here, so we cut across the town as quick as we could. Damn shame we weren't in time."

Sam got up and shook his hand. "I grieve for Maisy."

"You didn't do nothin' to help, though, did you?" Ethan spat as he looked up at Sam with malice.

"It all happened too quickly."

Ruth, who was beside Ethan said, "Sam stopped Strickland shooting the children. He couldn't have done anything about Maisy. None of us knew what she was going to do."

"Mrs. Gerber's right," Justin said, kneeling beside Ethan.

"I'd have stopped him," Ethan insisted, though with less conviction. "It ain't fair."

Ruth got to her feet, pulling the sobbing children away. Their clothes were stained with their mother's blood. "Come on, let's clean you up,".

"Who's gonna look after us now?" Kaitlin sobbed.

Ruth got onto her knees, so she was at the level of the children. "With God's help, we will. Samuel and I will look after you."

Samuel Gerber watched his wife leave with the two distraught children, then led Justin and Thomas out front to survey the damage before heading up the rise to begin digging.

19

Elijah

Day 4: Glendale, CA

Wade gasped as they emerged from the back street and looked up at the district police station in the early pre-dawn. "What the hell?"

Where the station had been was now a burned-out ruin, the air full of the stench of burned wood and melted plastic.

Here and there, small fires had been made in garbage cans, and figures picked among the trash by their flickering light.

Wade drew his weapon and moved forward, calling a warning to the looters. "Police! I'm giving one warning and one warning only."

Instantly the figures melted into the darkness, though Wade knew they'd be watching from the shadows. "Keep close," he said.

"Why are you going inside?" Becky hissed.

"I have to be certain about something," he replied, flicking on his Maglite before stepping between the blackened frame of the entrance and into the reception area, his boots cracking on shattered glass. Chairs had been ripped out and thrown across the floor, to be consumed in the flames. So, rioters had been in here before setting light to the place. He'd originally thought they might have lobbed Molotov cocktails in through the front door.

He reached the sergeant's desk, now a mess of tortured plastic and wood, with DeSantos's swivel chair now nothing more than a metal skeleton. The base of the desk was, however, intact, and he opened the bottom drawer to find a second flashlight. He switched it on, gave the Maglite to Becky, and swept the light across the scene, aware of watchers moving as the beam filled the shadows they were hiding in.

No one challenged him, however, as he made his way to the door between the public area and the offices beyond. The door had been forced but, if anything, the fire had been even more intense here and there was little to see except blackened wood and rubble from where the wall had collapsed.

"Let's get out of here," Becky said. "If they come after us, we could be trapped."

He put his hand up and led her to the pen. The metal bars still stood, but fire had swept through the holding cells, destroying everything inside. He paused outside one and ran the flashlight over the twisted ruins of the bed.

"Look," he said, pointing to a shape on the floor. "Lynch."

The body had been preserved in its final agonizing throes, like the victims of Pompeii. It looked to Wade as though Lynch had been at the bars, probably calling for someone to let him out when, finally, the flames forced him back until he fell to the floor unable to escape and perished. "Welcome to Hell," Wade said. He liked to think of himself as a compassionate man, in general, but he reserved that empathy for the victims of crime, not its perpetrators. For all the ruin of the past days, the world was a better place without Lynch in it.

Becky peered through the bars, careful not to touch them.

"I wanted you to see he's gone," Wade said. "Now, we can go." He'd seen enough dead bodies over the decades to not be too fazed by this one, especially knowing what the man had done, but even he was a little weirded out by the fact that he was wearing a coat he'd taken from Lynch's closet. The murderer was a little smaller than he was, so he couldn't quite close it at the front.

She nodded, her eyes wide, though without the disgust he'd expected of her. "Where?"

"To headquarters. If the city has a law enforcement presence, they'll likely regroup there."

He could see the disappointment in her eyes.

"Becky, I have to know what's happened here and whether there's a police department for me to belong to. If not, I'll be on the road east."

He didn't look back at the shriveled corpse in the cell, but despite the danger, he felt reassured that Lynch at least had received justice. On the other hand, if Sergeant DeSantos had been alive and capable, he'd have gotten Lynch out. He felt a chill as he thought of his friend and said a silent prayer that he'd escaped with his life. The only crumb of comfort was that, aside from Lynch, there were no bodies here, so likely they'd been able to evacuate. Unless, of course, they'd died here, and a police cleanup squad had been in since.

He led the way back out through the inner door, checking for movement before signaling for Becky to follow him.

He breathed a sigh of relief as they left the building behind and sheltered in the doorway of a residential building. The street outside the district station was littered with vehicles that had been stopped in their tracks when the EMP — if it had been an EMP — hit. The windows had been smashed on every one and, here and there, Wade could see human forms lying, unmoving.

Wade was confident that whatever had caused the radiation, it wasn't a human enemy. If the Chinese, Russians or North Koreans had attacked the US, they'd know about it by now. Los Angeles would be one of the top few targets for any invading force, especially if their enemy lay to the west.

That, however, was cold comfort if it meant that the whole of humanity had fallen. The fact that he'd seen no state level or federal response told him that this was widespread, almost certainly national in scope, and possibly global. How many had gotten sick? It depended on how long the radiation burst had lasted. If it was only a few hours, then it would only affect those parts of the Earth that had been facing that way at the time. If it was more than 24 hours, then it would have gotten to every part of the planet. And how many people would have resisted the temptation to go outside and look up when the dancing lights were in the sky? How many billions were now dead or gravely ill? He could only have been exposed for a short time, and yet he'd been unconscious for hours and he'd been looked after.

How many hadn't been killed by the initial dose, but would die from the longer-term effects over the coming weeks? Would he be among them?

They jogged along North Jackson Street, hugging the sides of the buildings, Wade's handgun held ready, eyes sweeping the shadows. He couldn't figure out why it was so quiet. There was evidence of rioting everywhere, but now the streets were largely deserted. Maybe the looters and rioters had signed their own death warrants by being outside under the dancing lights. Yes, that'd account for at least some of them. But surely not everyone. Though most of the stores they passed had smashed windows, they hadn't been entirely emptied. Surely if people were hiding in their homes, they'd want to venture out to get food? The skies were calm, after all. Unless people hadn't made the connection. In his decades as a cop, he'd concluded that most folks were pretty dumb.

"Hey, who the hell are you?"

Wade stopped short, cursing himself for allowing his mind to drift.

A big white man in a black sweatshirt was pointing a handgun at Wade. Around him stood half a dozen others and Wade's years of experience told him they were trouble.

Wade had had just enough presence of mind to slip his weapon into its holster before putting his hands up. "We're just passing through, brother," he said.

"Hey, nice one, bro!" the man said, smiling. "Good lookin' lady you got yourself." He lowered the gun a little, using it as if it were an extension of his hands.

Wade was just about to put him right when he felt Becky's arms run around his waist. Taking his cue from her, he lowered his arms. "Thanks. Now, you gonna let us pass through?"

The man glanced at his gang and shrugged. "I reckon you can go where you like, man. But me and this fine lady, we're gonna have a little talk. World is a different place right about now, and you gotta be close to someone who's gonna protect you."

"I am," Becky said, without a hint of fear in her voice.

The man laughed. "'dat right? Your man there, he put his hands up soon as he saw me. Now, you come to me girl and we make an arrangement."

Becky sneered. "No way. I got standards."

The man laughed again, but Wade detected an edge to it. This was getting dangerous.

And then, in an instant, his arm straightened, he brought the gun up and fired.

But Wade had seen it coming. Serving in the air force's special ops before joining the police, he still had razor-sharp reactions despite being in his mid-fifties.

If Becky hadn't been there, he'd have dropped the thug, but as it was he wasted milliseconds pushing her clear before he fell to his knee and brought his Colt to bear.

The gang leader had just enough time to react, and the round fizzed past, taking out the man beside him who'd leaped to his feet as he saw his boss making his move.

As he swerved to one side, the gang leader fired three rounds, but Wade had flung himself away, finding shelter behind an abandoned truck, Becky cowering beside him.

"I'm sorry!" she cried out over the crack and ping of gunfire.

"You've been watching too much TV," Wade said as he took aim and fired. His weapon had a nine-round magazine and one in the chamber, so he was taking single shots and counting them down.

The gang leader had taken cover within the doorway of the mechanic shop he'd been standing outside when he'd seen Wade. The others were nearby, and Wade knew that if any of them outflanked him, he'd have no chance, so he kept the pressure on with regular, accurate shots.

"Becky, pull the magazine out of my back pocket," he said. He was going to have to reload quickly once he took his last shot.

And then, as he glanced across at her to take the new magazine, they rushed him. Afterward, he guessed at least some of them must have been drunk or high because it was a suicidal move. The leader was at the back, lumbering forward while his subordinates took the heat.

Wade slipped the magazine into place. They were feet away. He took out the first, then swung his weapon to the left as a lean black man bore down on him. Becky cried out in terror.

Then the black man fell forward as a round took him in the back.

"This is the police. Drop your weapons!"

The voice was being broadcast from a megaphone, but the gang paid it no heed, their momentum taking them toward Wade and Becky.

"Drop!" he called, pulling her down with him.

The deep throated thunks of high caliber weapons filled the air, followed by yells of pain and then, as Wade lay flat on the ground, the fat head of the gang leader flopped down, his sightless eyes looking directly into Wade's.

"Remain still!" A voice instructed from above, then Wade felt his arms being pulled together as he and Becky were hauled up.

Wade let out a huge breath as the police officer, dressed in black body armor, spun him around and pushed him back onto the hood of the car.

"I'm a detective," Wade said.

"Sure you are, buddy."

"Detective Elijah Wade, Glendale PD. My badge is in my pocket."

The young officer's flushed excitement dissipated instantly as he nodded to his colleague who frisked Wade.

Then a familiar uniformed figure appeared around the vehicle.

"Chief," Wade said. What did they say about cockroaches being the only survivors of nuclear Armageddon? Roaches and Deputy Chief of Police Marshall McKinney.

"Detective Wade. Of course *you'd* survive. Though not for much longer if we hadn't arrived." McKinney was a thin man with a close-shaven mustache. He looked like a bank teller, but Wade knew him to be ruthless.

"I appreciate the assist, Chief. Can you give me any news on Sergeant DeSantos and the rest of the team?"

McKinney shook his head. "I'm not your secretary, Detective. Report to the police department for assignment. We have much to do, and we need all the help we can get. Even yours."

\#

He found Joe DeSantos almost as soon as he arrived at the police headquarters building. The sergeant's obvious relief and surprise mirrored his own as they embraced.

"Thank God," DeSantos said. "I thought for sure you were dead. Jeez, it's good to see you."

"How's Terry?"

Wade could tell from his expression what DeSantos was going to say. "I'm sorry, Elijah. We lost him, and Jenkins — they died before we could get them to the hospital. Then, as soon as the sky-lights went out, we got attacked by looters.

Had to abandon the station and make my way here or we'd have been burned alive."

"It's okay, Joe. I should have been there."

"This Becky?" DeSantos said, looking beyond Wade.

"Yeah."

"Then you did the right thing."

Wade put his arm around the sergeant's shoulder and guided him to a quiet corner. "Lynch was still in his cell when you left?"

"Yeah. I should have gotten him out, but by that time I couldn't get to the pen."

"It's okay, Joe. I just wanted to be sure he was in there — I've been to the station and saw a burned body in his cell."

DeSantos shrugged. "Well, unless some fool let him out and then put another body inside, I guess we can say he's dead."

"Sure. I'd want dental records in normal times, but I figure those days are over. Can you give me a rundown?"

DeSantos glanced at Becky. "Of course, but you'd better take Becky to the ghetto. She won't be able to come inside."

"The ghetto?"

"It's what we call the safe area. It's in the old civic center across the street. You'd best see one of the LTs to get a full briefing, but I can give you a summary."

Wade nodded, pulling the man closer so they could speak without being overheard.

"So, you remember the chief gave that order on the radio just before you headed out?"

"Yeah."

"Well, everything went to hell pretty quickly. The radio stopped working, so we just had to hunker down and keep the station secure. But Terry was real sick by then, so I was getting ready to carry him and Jenkins to the hospital when we came under attack. We couldn't hold them back and then they started using firebombs and I knew it was up. We had no way to get reinforcements and the world had gone to hell.

"Terry died as we tried to get away, so I led the survivors here. The chief's dead, so McKinney's in charge now, and we're restoring order block by block centered on here. McKinney's put a curfew in place, and he leads enforcement squads out onto the streets to keep the peace. Word is the National Guard is working with police in LA, so we hope they'll be here soon. For now, though, it's just about survival."

"What about helping civilians?"

DeSantos tilted his head apologetically. "If they come here, we help them, but we can't go looking for people. We're holding on by our fingernails as it is, Elijah. Now, why don't you go find Becky somewhere safe and you can lend a hand. We sure as hell need you."

20

Elijah

"Hey Wade, you son of a bitch!"

Elijah had just made his way into the open plan CIU office when he heard the familiar voice calling. "Larry. Glad to see you made it."

Detective Lorenzo Costa took his hand and shook it vigorously. "I should'a known you'd make it. Man, it's good to see you."

"You too."

"Where've you been?"

"Working a case."

"Ha! Typical. Cracked it? Justice done?"

Wade nodded. "We got lucky and caught the Cleaner. I went after Becky Powell, you know, his last victim."

"And you found her?"

"I did."

Costa shook his head. "I got to hand it to you, Lige, you're one of a kind. What happened to the Cleaner?"

"Died in his cell when the station was burned down."

"Good. I wonder how long it'll be before we're working cases again. We're just keeping the peace here."

"Only until the National Guard deploys, I hear."

"That's the official line, but I haven't seen any sign of them. Want a coffee?"

"I do, but I've got to report to the LT."

Costa grunted. "She's one of the good ones. Maybe the only one left."

"Yeah, I met McKinsey already."

Slapping him on the shoulder, Costa raised his finger to his lips and then headed off, disappearing into his cubicle.

Wade knocked on the door marked Supervisor and waited until he was called in.

"Detective, it's good to see you."

"LT, likewise."

Lieutenant Carey Bullock's smile was obviously genuine, but she couldn't hide the exhaustion in her eyes.

"I don't have a specific assignment for you, but I'll work one out."

"Thanks. Any chance of a summary of the strategic picture?"

Now the smile warmed a little. "You mean what the frak is going on? Sure. And it'll only cost you a coffee."

Wade nodded and headed to the machine in the staff cafeteria. Carey Bullock was the best of the senior officers in the department, but she lacked the political skill of a career officer, which made her the ideal source of BS-free information.

He returned to the supervisor's office and put the Styrofoam cup down.

"Thanks. Take a seat," she said.

Wade sat and sipped at his coffee as she got up and gestured at the map of the city. "Our current operations are focused on securing this area around the department headquarters before spreading outward until we have full control again. That's the theory, anyway."

"You don't sound confident."

"Policing, even as ... vigorous ... as this, depends on the support of a justice system that the majority of the public believe in. If all you've got is the threat and use of force, you're going to be vulnerable if someone comes along with a bigger capability."

"Like who?"

She shrugged. "I don't know, but we lost eighty percent of our headcount on day one, dead or wounded. Now, we have no idea how many people in the city are dead, but we haven't got enough boots to control the entire area. We're going to reach a limit and be unable to go any further."

"How's John?" John was her husband, a detective in LAPD.

"Alive, as far as I know. He got a message to me. But ..." she trailed off as she slumped in her seat. "Like everyone else, I haven't been able to get in touch with my daughter. I try not to think about what's happened to her and her kids."

Wade let out a deep breath. "I feel you. Kelly's in New York. She was having an operation on the night it all happened. Look, Carey, I've got a long journey ahead of me." He took the badge out of his pocket and slid it onto the desk.

"No can do, Elijah. You can't abandon your city when it needs you."

"I can't abandon my daughter, either. I wish to God I hadn't prioritized the department so much over the years. I should have been with her in the hospital."

Bullock downed her coffee. "I know how you feel, really I do. I could say exactly the same myself. But you're here, not there, and we can't afford to lose someone like you."

"Like me?"

She leaned forward. "I know you've got no love for McKinsey, and I also know you're one of the few people who'd stand up to him if he went too far."

"So would you."

"Yeah, but I need backup."

"What do you think he's likely to do?"

"I don't know, but some of the general orders we've been given are turning us from a police force to vigilantes."

"These are desperate times, LT."

"Sure, but we both know our history well enough to know that the worst despots hide behind preserving security so they can grab more and more power. He thinks he's the only man who can restore order and run the city.

The mayor's handed over day to day control. I need you to stay, Elijah. Back me up. Things will come to a head pretty soon and I'll need all the help I can get when the time comes. Please."

Elijah groaned. It was bad enough that he knew he had a long journey ahead of him, but it would take even longer if it was delayed. But she was right. He couldn't abandon his brothers and sisters, or the people of the city he'd sworn to protect.

"Okay," he said. "I'll stick around for a day or two."

Bullock smiled and pushed his badge back at him. "Good. McKinsey has banned resignations anyway. We're a conscripted service now."

"Why didn't you say that in the first place?"

"Because I need to know you're on my side, not that you're staying because otherwise he'd have you shot. Now, take a few hours break and find a billet. The duty roster will be posted later. It's good to have you back, Elijah."

He took the badge, nodded and left the room.

#

Wade's mood darkened further as he made his way through the department building. The place had the feel of a castle under siege. They'd obviously gotten the generators running, but half the officers he saw wore the dazed expressions of men and women trying to cope with a tsunami of grief at the loss of loved ones. The loss of a world. It would be post-traumatic stress disorder except that they were still in the middle of the trauma, with no end in sight.

Whole floors had been cleared and turned into temporary accommodation, and he saw rows of exhausted people lying on salvaged mattresses, some apparently asleep, others talking in whispers to each other.

He'd worked in this and other department buildings for decades, and they'd each had a life of their own. Here, that life had gone. The people here were simply surviving, with no vision of a future, let alone any hope that it would come about.

For now, however, he was most worried about Becky. She'd been through a special kind of hell on top of the one they were all experiencing. She hadn't told him how she'd come to be captured by Lynch or what he did to her, but he suspected those memories would come to the surface sooner rather than later. After risking his life to save hers, the last thing he wanted was for her to do anything destructive. He had a feeling that the course of their lives would run together for some time and, while he didn't relish the burden that imposed on him, he couldn't abandon her.

He greeted DeSantos on the first floor, then emerged onto the street outside the police department building. The bright morning had given way to more typical December weather, and he pulled Lynch's coat around his shoulders before crossing the road to the old community center building. He was surprised by how many people were moving back and forth along the pavement. Many of them were carrying boxes and pieces of furniture and he realized they were systematically stripping the neighboring buildings of anything useful. They reminded him of an ant colony on the move.

He flashed his badge to the guards at the entrance before moving into the relative darkness inside. The community center had been converted into a complex of workshops for small businesses, but the only light came from the tall windows in all the walls.

"Elijah!"

Becky threw her arms around him and hugged him tight. "I thought you'd left me!"

"Why would you think that? I told you I'd be back."

She shook her head. "I dunno. I was just scared. Maria here, she said you'd come back."

"Didn't believe it, if I'm honest," the young woman Becky had been sitting with said. "Glad to see I was wrong.

And right."

"Let's get something to eat," Wade said.

Maria pointed along the hall. "You line up along there. Caviar and steak's on the menu today."

"Smartass," Wade muttered as they headed away. "She should be grateful she's safe here."

Becky gripped his arm and hissed into his ear. "Her husband's dead and she doesn't know where her kids are."

Well, that certainly made Wade feel like a complete idiot. He couldn't begin to comprehend the magnitude of the misery that his fellow humans were experiencing. His parents were both dead and the only living relatives he cared about were his daughter Kelly and (in the privacy of his own mind) his ex-wife, Lindsay. Not knowing whether they were alive or, indeed, whether he'd ever know either way for sure, was torture, but at least there was a chance they were okay. Maria had already experienced greater hurt than he had.

"I'm sorry," he said.

Becky squeezed his arm. "It's okay. I know you're a good guy really."

They joined the end of the line, and Wade groaned. "I can't believe how many people there are here."

"They feel safer here, so they put up with spending their lives lining up, whether it's food, washing or sanitation. How long are we staying?"

Wade shrugged, taking in the mass of humanity crammed into such a small space. It made him think of concentration camps and long-distance space flight. He chuckled. To think humanity had been planning a return to the moon. And the Perseverance rover on Mars would be waiting a long time for its next instruction set.

The food, when they got it, was fine — Wade had certainly experienced worse in the military and he wondered where it had come from. Liberated from grocery stores, he supposed. For now, at least, it seemed that food wasn't going to be the main problem.

The next line was the one for accommodation. After an hour, they made it to the front, sitting down opposite a young woman who looked as though the end of her tether was in the rearview mirror.

"I'm sorry, I don't have anything left, except for kids or the old and infirm."

Wade sighed. "Couldn't you have put a sign up? Saved us waiting?"

"Why, you got somewhere else you got to go?"

"I'll be on duty soon enough." He showed her his badge.

"Police? Then you'd best find somewhere to crash in the police department building opposite."

"Becky isn't in the police, just me."

The woman shrugged. "There's plenty of rule bending going on. But look, if you want something off-grid, if you take my meaning, you should check out the high school, two blocks from here. There's plenty of room in there, I hear, and it's inside the ring. Just about. You can come back here for your meals."

Remembering his misjudgment of Maria, Wade thanked the woman and led Becky through the crowd. He pulled her to one side. "What do you think? You can either hang around here, or we can try to find somewhere else."

"Let's check out the school."

"You know I've got to go on duty soon?"

She nodded. "I figured that. I'm glad you're sticking around to help, and I reckon I'll be easier to find at the school than among so many people."

"I just hope my apartment hasn't been trashed," he said as they made their way toward the door. It was a long way outside the protective cordon but, on the other hand, it wasn't exactly a prime target. It was on the top floor of a small apartment block, and, from the outside, it looked more like an emergency exit than anything. But if he was to go east, he'd need to go back there first.

They were just heading out of the old civic center building when a voice called out.

"Detective!"

"Hi Joe."

"Lieutenant Bullock asked me to track you down. You've been assigned to one of the spearpoint units."

"What are they?"

DeSantos shook his head. "We call them the suicide squads. They go in to clear out an area. You know, to widen the ring."

"I thought we were waiting for the National Guard."

"You know McKinsey. Anyway, you're to report to the level one briefing room at sixteen hundred."

Wade grunted. "Well, McKinsey didn't waste any time, did he? Day one and I'm on a suicide mission."

DeSantos slapped him on the shoulder. "Sorry, Lige. But I reckon you can handle it."

"Do me a solid and find Becky somewhere to stay, will you? We've been told there's space in the high school."

"Sure. The least I can do. Come on, kid."

He didn't look back, but he knew she was watching him as he crossed to the department building.

21

Elijah

"So, what did you do to get under McKinsey's skin?"

Elijah had walked into the briefing room to find a small group of uniformed officers — four men and two women — sitting behind a horseshoe-shaped arrangement of desks. Two were cleaning and checking their carbines, the parts spread over the desk, others were talking together in low voices.

The man who'd spoken was a little younger than Wade — late forties he'd guess — and was standing in front of a whiteboard.

Wade smiled. "Oh, me and the chief go way back."

"You must be Detective Wade," the man said, crossing the room and holding out his hand in greeting. "I'm Sergeant Chris Williams, though I prefer Chip. Or Sarge."

"Elijah Wade, first district."

"Military service?"

Wade nodded. "Six years in the Airforce Special Operations Wing. Last couple on diplomatic protection. Long time ago now, though."

"I was just a grunt, but you never lose it, do you?"

"So, what's this all about?"

"Ever seen that movie *The Expendables*? Well, that's us, except without the big budget. What you see here is the spearpoint, half a dozen officers — present and past — who are all unsuited to peacetime policing, but ideal for the end of the world. At least, that's what McKinsey said to me. It's not exactly a coincidence that every single person he's assigned to the team had a beef with him of some kind."

"Including you?"

Williams shrugged. "Yeah. I got retired from LAPD a few years ago rather than go on trial for, basically, following orders. McKinsey wanted to throw me under the bus, but he didn't get his own way and he had to take his share of the flack. That's why he was never elected chief. Or so he thinks. Lucky for him Chief Feeney's dead and the mayor's a sniveling coward. The city's run by McKinsey, heaven help it."

"So, why are you doing this?" Wade asked, gesturing at the others, some of whom were obviously listening in.

"Because McKinsey might be bad, but he's nothing on what would happen if we lose control. Best case scenario would be chaos. Worst case, gang rule. I've lost enough these past days; I won't stand by and watch everything go to hell. Course, you might see things differently, and I need to know whether you're on my team or not."

"Do I have a choice?"

"Sure. But I have to know who I can trust when the brown stuff hits the fan. Can I count on you?"

Wade nodded. "I'm a man of my word."

"Good. Then let me introduce your fellow expendables." he said, pointing out each of them as he spoke their names. "Hooper, Cheng, Varela, Fitch and Kowalski — take my advice and don't turn your back on her."

He was rewarded with the middle finger from a woman who was cleaning her weapon. She didn't look up at either of them, but Wade could tell from the way she worked on her carbine that she was very familiar with firearms.

"Kowalski's former Israeli secret services. The rest of us are current or former beat officers, and all military veterans. We know how to handle ourselves, but there's just not enough of us. We lost Ruby yesterday. Now, we've got to prepare for tonight's mission."

Wade shook hands with each of his new teammates. He was the oldest by some margin, and he suspected that some of them didn't rate him as a decent replacement for Ruby, whoever he or she was. To be frank, he felt pretty much the same way, but he could handle himself, and leave the younger ones to do any jumping around.

He took a seat next to Kowalski who, by this time, had finished reassembling her weapon, and paid attention to Williams. They were to clear out the Wells Fargo branch a few blocks away. It was, Williams said, of tactical importance because, once it was secure, their cordon would be complete one block farther out than before. Wade, on the other hand, was pretty certain it was no coincidence that they were being sent in to clear out a bank. Even after the apocalypse, money talked.

"What about the lights?" one of the others asked. "We got any Geiger counters yet?"

Williams shook his head. "No. We'll have to stick with the patches for now. Look, I know it's not ideal …"

"Not ideal? Seriously, do they want us to die out there?"

The second woman turned to the speaker. "You know the answer to that question. As long as we've done our job, McKinsey'd be happy for us to … disappear."

Putting his hands up to silence them, Williams said, "At least we know the patches work." Seeing Wade's puzzled expression, he walked over and handed what looked like an armband to him. "Photoluminescent paint glows when the lights are out. Wear this on your forearm, but inside out otherwise it won't be the radiation that kills you. Anyway," he continued, speaking to the whole team, "a Geiger counter's not going to be much use unless it's modified. So, we make do. We've all been cops or soldiers for long enough to be used to that."

The grumbles dwindled as the police officers nodded. It was a universal truth that there was never enough money for the equipment they needed so they could keep up with the criminals, let alone get ahead of them. It was just the same in the military. Out of date weapons and armor; even more out of date tactics.

They were to reconvene a couple of hours later, but while the others left to get food and, perhaps, a little shut-eye, Wade elected to talk to Kowalski, who was now stripping down her handgun.

"Nice piece," he said. "Sig?"

"P229."

"Three fifty-seven?"

For the first time, she actually looked at him. "Forty caliber," she said, sliding the barrel back into place. "Small hands."

He sat and watched her for a moment, content to let her control the conversation. She put the gun down and gestured at him. "What do you carry?" she asked in a subtle Israeli accent.

"1911, Bureau," he said, pulling the weapon out and laying it on the table.

"Nice. Forty-five?"

"Yeah. Bigger, but slower, like me."

She chuckled at that, transforming her hard features for a moment.

"Were you in the FBI?"

Now it was his turn to laugh. "Not me. I just like their weapons. You were special forces?"

"Shayetet 13."

He knew better than to ask why she'd left. "I was Air Force special services. But that was a long time ago."

She paused for a moment, and then looked at him. "Why are you talking to me? Nobody else does."

"Because I learned a long time ago to find the best soldier in a squad and stick with him. Or her."

Her eyebrow arched. "How do you know I am the best?"

"Call it instinct, call it experience, if you like."

She grunted. "Just don't slow me down, old man."

#

In December, the sun went down early, and with it came the curfew. As Wade followed the others along Wilson Avenue, he wondered what the date was. Was it Christmas Eve? But he couldn't afford the mental resources to work it out right now.

He flipped the patch on his forearm and saw that there was no sign of any glow. Maybe they'd seen the last of the lights. They'd done enough damage, for sure. Humanity might take decades to recover. But, if the lights returned, then they were facing an extinction level event. A sterilization of the planet.

His spider sense had been tingling since they'd emerged into the darkness. Last night's near silence had been replaced by an almost inaudible background noise. It was as if the city was waking up rather than settling down for the night as it ought to have been. But, aside from this non-silence, only occasional sounds punctuated the night: windows shattering, the crack of gunshot. Never close at hand, but he felt the city closing in on him, and his eyes searched the shadows for danger.

Despite her sneering tone, Kowalski was jogging along at his side, as they ran in double file with Williams and Cheng in the lead. Kowalski and Wade were in the rear, and he saw her snap around every now and again to check behind them, her carbine sweeping the darkness. They were relying on diffused moonlight to navigate, along with the occasional still-burning fire farther off in the distance and reflecting on the windows of the office buildings.

They paused for a moment outside a Seventh Day Adventist church. Like most of the "safe" area within the cordon, it had no power, but he could see the flickering of candles through the windows and hear gentle singing over the sound of his own heavy breathing.

"You okay, Wade?" Kowalski asked.

He nodded. "I could do with a smoke. Trying not to slow you down. And call me Elijah, or Lige, will you?"

She shrugged. "You can call me Kowalski."

She either had a sense of humor drier than the Mojave, or she had no sense of humor at all. And then she gave a tiny smile. "Mira. My name is Mira. But don't tell the others."

"I won't, I promise. What are we waiting for, do you think?"

"The sergeant is talking with Cheng. They are, like, joined at the hip. But they are also careful, so I approve. You okay?"

Wade looked back along the way they'd come. "I don't know. I can't help shaking this feeling."

"What kind of feeling?"

"I wish I could say for sure. But I've learned to trust my gut over the years, and it says something's wrong."

"Maybe you're just nervous."

"Oh, I'm nervous alright. It's bad enough that we've got to clear out an unknown number of gang members, but ... I mean, Wells Fargo?"

She sighed. "Williams says it has tactical value."

"And it's also as far away from the police department as we can get without being outside the cordon."

"But that is the point. By taking the bank, we complete the perimeter. It will be easier to hold, then. And we're not the only spearpoint operation tonight. We're just the one with the farthest target."

He leaned back against the railing and, yet again, checked his 1911. "You're probably right. Maybe I'm just nervous."

"Nervous is good," she said. "Stay nervous, stay alive. Come on."

They followed the others along the street until they reached a corner where Williams called them together. "The building is fifty yards that way. Varela and Fitch, make your way to your positions, then signal. When we open fire, you're to follow. You've got ten minutes. Understood?"

They nodded, glanced at the others for a moment, and then flitted into the darkness, across the intersection and instantly lost.

Williams gathered them all together. "I want this to go like clockwork. Don't forget Ruby. Got cocky and lost his head. We go in hard and fast. Oh, and Wade, this is a military operation, understood?"

"No prisoners, sarge."

"No prisoners. Unless they're harmless, of course. But be sure. We've got the jump on them, but they'll outnumber us. Let's see this through and we can all enjoy some R&R tomorrow."

As the time crept by, Wade thought he heard the sound level in the distance go up a notch. He looked across at Kowalski who didn't seem to have noticed, so he tried to put it out of his mind. Do this job, help secure the city and then he could travel across the country to find his daughter with a clear conscience. Or, as clear as it was ever going to be. He hadn't been there, and nothing he did now would erase that shame. He touched the mermaid pendant that hung from his neck.

"That's the signal!" Kowalski said, tapping him on the arm.

He brought his carbine to eye level and followed the others, wishing for the hundredth time that the police department had invested in night sights. But the glow of fires was stronger here, and his old eyes more acclimatized, so he kept pace with the others until they reached the edge of a building overlooking their target.

"No sign of any activity," Williams hissed over his shoulder.

"Maybe they know we're coming."

That bad feeling that had been gnawing at Wade got even worse. If he were commanding this mission, he'd regroup, order a full reconnaissance and only once he knew the enemy's complete disposition would he go in. But Williams was an action-taker and he was also exhausted, Wade suspected. The man wanted tonight over as quickly as possible, so he was going to see the situation through that lens. After all, maybe Wade *was* being over-cautious. They were heavily armed, and their opponents were just street scum with, likely, one controlling mind. Take him, or her, out and they would be finished.

"Where are Varela and Fitch?" he whispered to Kowalski.

"Across the street," she said, moving her head sideways. "At least, I hope so. I'm beginning to think you might have been right about this. Be careful when we go in."

"Kowalski, Wade, take the left. When you hear us open fire, come in weapons hot."

"Yes, Sarge," Kowalski said. "Good hunting."

Williams nodded to the two of them, but Wade could see the uncertainty in his face. This wasn't going like the other, successful, raids.

Breaking cover, Wade followed Kowalski as she hugged the side of a building, dark against the faint orange glow.

They passed across the front entrance of a Staples, hiding momentarily in the palm trees outside, fog rising from them as the caught their breath. Wade tried to ignore the scent of urine and stale cigarettes that wafted out of the vegetation as he scanned the Wells Fargo. To their left was a covered parking area beneath a mall he could just see above it. Beyond, he could see the moon emerging from behind a cloud to illuminate the distant hills.

But it was the perfect black of the parking lot's yawning opening that drew his attention. Anyone could be hiding in there, ready to fire on them as soon as they moved out of cover.

Kowalski followed his gaze. "Yeah. We'd better get across there quickly."

"There's cover there and there," he said, pointing at a burned-out truck and sedan that were partially blocking the road. Power or no power, those vehicles must have been like honey to a bee to the looters.

"Jeez," he said as the moonlight exposed the prone forms of corpses: two under the truck and two more sprawled across the road.

Kowalski patted him on the arm. "I know, but we've got a job to do. We can't help the dead. Come on."

She jumped over the low brick wall and onto the sidewalk. Wade followed her, moving as quickly as he could, while charting a path so he'd be behind the vehicles for as long as possible. Any moment now he expected to hear the crack of gunfire and feel the searing, hot pain of a hit.

But it didn't happen. They reached the temporary safety of a taller stand of palm trees that stood directly outside the Wells Fargo door. He was beginning to wonder if this was all some sort of trick. A wild goose chase.

Or a diversion.

Then gunfire and muzzle flashes split the night and instinct took over. He shouldered his carbine and took out his 1911, skirting around the front of the building and barely noticing the blackened Brinks truck on the main street.

Kowalski was just behind him, her Sig held beside her nose as she flitted past, drawing him to follow in her wake.

More gunfire. This time it was the unmistakable percussive punch of an assault weapon — hopefully one of their teams'. The reflecting flashes helped them make their way past the interview cubicles and into the main hall of the bank. The crowd control barrier had been kicked over, and Wade hugged the shattered glass of the counter as the room filled with the stench of gunfire along with the underlying smell of something else, something rotten.

Kowalski patted Wade on the shoulder and pointed to an open door leading to the back office. That was where the sound and smell was coming for.

Keeping a couple of yards apart, they kept low as they ran across the hall.

As they reached the door, a voice boomed out. "Drop your weapons. We got your people."

Peering through the gap between the door and hinge, Kowalski and Wade could make out what looked like a war zone, smoke drifting in the air, swirling in the diffuse fire light as figures moved.

"Dammit!" Kowalski said. "They got Williams."

"I know you're out there. Two of you, I figure. We got your number. Come and join the party."

Wade could make out the slumped figure of the sergeant and, beside him, other bodies. Then someone cried out in pain.

"That's Fitch. Goddamit! They suckered us."

"I give you ten, and then we kill them all."

"They're going to kill us whatever we do, you know that," Wade said.

"Nine."

"If we give them the chance. The sarge is dead, and so are the others. Fitch is going to follow them."

"The question is whether we give ourselves up."

"Eight."

"We both know the answer to that."

Wade nodded and swung his carbine off his shoulder. He disengaged the safety and locked eyes with Kowalski. "We could just run for it."

"Seven."

She smiled.

"No, I didn't think so.

"Six."

They raised their weapons and, as one ran into the hall, hugging the walls, sweeping around for targets, expecting at any instant a cacophony of gunfire.

There was nothing. Williams lay on the floor with his hands tied, blood soaking his jacket. Beside him, Cheng was obviously dead. Fitch was suspended from a light fitting, arms bound with razor wire.

"Five."

"Where's the voice coming from?"

"Ambush," Williams said. "Get out of here."

"Four."

"What?"

"GET OUT OF HERE! That's an order! Bomb!"

"Three."

With one look at Kowalski, Wade grabbed her by the arm and, together, they ran.

"Two."

They'd barely passed through the doorway to the back office when ...

"One."

The blast took Wade's feet out from under him, the ear-splitting roar combining with the tearing rumble of the building's roof falling in, enveloping him in dust, concrete and blood.

And then it all went dark.

22

Elijah

"Wade! Wake up, damn you!"

He could barely hear her voice over the buzzing in his ears. The room seemed to be shaking. And then he realized it wasn't the room, it was him.

He spat out a mouthful of dust and rubble, wrapping his fingers around the hand that was thrust down to him.

"What ... what happened?"

"We walked into a trap. You saved my life — another second and both of us would be dead now. McKinsey wanted to tidy up all his loose ends in one go, I think."

"But what about the gang here?"

"Nonexistent, I guess. Someone knew exactly what our tactics would be and used that to ambush the others, then drew us in. Lucky for us we were the last inside."

Wade got clumsily to his feet. A mixture of moonlight and the orange flicker of fires illuminated the unrecognizable chaos the bomb had caused. The internal walls had all been torn apart and left in shreds, coated in dust and splintered wood.

"Can you walk?" Kowalski said as she brushed herself down and regarded him doubtfully.

"Yeah."

"You're bleeding."

She was pointing at the red stain on his arm. It hurt like hell, but he couldn't feel running blood. "It's a graze. I'm okay, honestly. But what should we do? Back to the station?"

"I don't see that we have a choice. But not through the front door — McKinsey is certain to have lookouts. We need to wait until someone comes out."

"Then what?"

She shrugged as she dug around for her carbine. "Who knows? Get out of Dodge, I suppose."

"Well, I guess I'm now officially retired," Wade said. "But we can't let McKinsey get away with killing our friends."

"They weren't my friends."

"Comrades, then."

She brushed the dust off her weapon and checked it before putting it over her shoulder.

"You're limping," Wade said, noticing for the first time.

"So are you. I'll walk it off. I just hope the ringing in my ears passes sooner rather than later."

"So, what about McKinsey? Are you going to help me? He wanted you dead, too."

They picked their way through the rubble before emerging onto the street again. Wade saw shapes scurrying for cover as he scanned for danger.

"I don't go looking for revenge," she said.

Wade glanced at her. "And that's a lie."

"Okay, then. I pick my fights carefully. McKinsey has the city in his pocket and, anyway, if we kill him, how does that help?"

They moved across the road as quickly as they could, then rested for a moment in a covered doorway.

"It's a question of justice," Wade said.

"Look, Elijah," she said, using his name for the first time. "Let me ask you this. Have you got anything, or anyone, to live for?"

As he looked out of the shadows, searching for trouble, he wondered what he should tell her. "I rescued a young woman from a serial killer on the night everything went to hell. She's my responsibility. And then there's my daughter, Kelly. But she's in New York."

She looked at him thoughtfully. "So, you're going to travel east? That's a long journey. For all we know, there are no working vehicles between here and there."

"I know. But I've got to try."

"Then leave McKinsey to me."

"What?"

"You've got this woman and your daughter — I reckon that'll keep you alive and motivated for a while. Me, I've got nothing."

He shook his head. "Of course you have."

"You're sweet, Elijah, but you don't know me. This is the end of the world, so what hope is there? Without hope, like you say, there is only justice. Now, let's move."

They slipped into the open, flitting from shadow to shadow until they were crouching under the railings of the Seventh Day Adventist church.

"So, where is your friend, this woman you rescued?" Kowalski asked.

"She should be at the high school — that's where I told her to go."

She nodded. "Then we'll have to split up soon. You head to the school then get yourself out of the city."

"What are you going to do?"

"Get revenge."

"How?"

"I'll watch and wait. And when he thinks he's gotten away with it, I'll blow his head off."

"Come away with us. I could use your help."

"Three's a crowd, Elijah."

"Not in this case. Becky's coming with me until we find somewhere safe for her. She has no concept how far it is on foot."

Kowalski grunted. "Neither do you. But McKinsey must pay. Even in the ruins, there must be justice. And who knows how many others will die at his hands if he's not stopped? *Laazazel!* we cannot let that scum live."

"Okay, I'll come with you. We'll deal with McKinsey and then get out of the city."

She shook her head. "No. You have responsibility for another. What happens to this Becky if you get killed? It is likely enough, after all. McKinsey is paranoid at the best of times, but after tonight, he'll surround himself."

"Then I'll find somewhere safe for her and come back to help you."

"Come on, my new friend. Where is safe now? She is safer with you than not with you. No, we must part. Maybe I will succeed and catch up with you. Which route are you taking?"

"I don't have a clue."

Kowalski looked back and forth along the street. "I would go north, then west from Sacramento on Route 80."

Wade hadn't considered going north first — in his mind's eye he'd imagined travelling west and then veering north once he was closing in. But by heading north through California first, he was making the start of the journey easier — at least in theory. He could tackle the mountains and deserts of the West and Midwest later. "Sure. Might as well."

She turned to him and grasped his hand. "*Leich l'shalom*, go with peace, Elijah Wade."

And she was gone, before he could respond. She launched herself away into the shadows and all he could do was whisper a prayer for her as she disappeared.

He felt an unaccountable sadness as he crouched there alone in the darkness. He knew that his chances of ever seeing her again were vanishingly small — even if she succeeded in her mission (and he wouldn't like to be in McKinsey's shoes when she caught up with him) then there was no practical way she could hope to find him in the vastness of the American continent.

But, right now, his priority had to be Becky. If McKinsey had been behind the attack — and his every instinct told him he was — then Wade could expect no mercy if he was discovered alive. He had to find Becky, and get them both out of the city before the hunt went up. He wasn't safe in the police-secured area, and he wasn't safe in the far larger zone that, at best, the authorities tried to keep in curfew. They would depend upon being invisible and being fast.

As he left the church behind, he took a left, sticking to the darkest shadows, his 1911 held close to his chest. The high school was within the cordon, but if he wasn't careful, he might run into a patrol or a marauding gang, and both would be bad news.

His leg had stiffened up as they'd run from the bank, but of all the oddness of this new world, it was the lack of any emergency service response to the explosion that freaked him out the most. It was as if it were a demolition job rather than a bomb which, in a way, he supposed it was.

The street turned from commercial to suburban as he ran, leafless trees in front of low-walled ranch houses replacing the soulless workshops and offices. He could see flickering lights inside some, but most were dark: abodes of the dead.

"Hey, you!" a voice called out.

Wade froze then very slowly rotated himself until he was facing an old man holding what looked like an antique revolver in shaking hands.

"You police, ain't you?"

A lifetime of habit made the word 'yes' form in his throat, but he chewed it back and spat out a 'no'.

The old man looked puzzled. "You sure look like one. National Guard? No? You sure as hell ain't from no gang I ever heard of." He lowered the weapon.

"What do you want?"

"Will you help me with my wife?"

The man looked so pitifully forlorn, that Wade found himself following him along the path to the ranch house he'd emerged from. "I'm not a doctor," he called. "I don't know how I can help."

"Just you follow me, son," he said, disappearing through the front door.

Wade reeled from the stench of death as he went inside. "What the hell?"

The old man turned to him in the dark hallway, lit only by a guttering candle. "She died on the first day. Laid there lookin' out the window at the beautiful lights. Said they was callin' her home."

"I'm sorry," Wade said. "But what do you want from me?"

"I can't rest 'til she gets a decent burial, but I can't lift her on my own."

He wanted to refuse, but the desperation in the man's face melted his resolve. Even as he stood there, still dusty and hurt from the bomb that had almost killed him, ears ringing, he knew that between yes and no lay his remaining humanity. If he was to expect to find a vestige of compassion on his journey across the country and into the future, he must begin by showing a little now, even though it would delay and disgust him.

The woman had been wrapped in a stained blanket and, even though the old man opened the windows wide, the stench only grew stronger as he got closer.

Taking most of the weight himself, he maneuvered the shrouded body down the stairs with as much respect and care as possible. Heaving it along the hallway and out through the door.

"Good God, how did you manage that?" he said as he saw the trench the old man had dug, running along the low fence.

"I began the night she died," he said. "Couldn't get it deep enough nearer the house."

Together, they dragged the body into the hole, and Wade waited, breathing heavily, as the old man stood at the makeshift graveside. It wasn't the regulation six feet deep, but it would do.

Wade tried not to listen as the old man said a prayer to his dead love, before turning to him, tears soaking his face. "Thank you, son," he said. "And I sure am sorry, I got to do this."

He raised the revolver and shot, the round going wide and smashing a window. He didn't get another chance. Wade's bullet took him in the upper chest, and he collapsed to his knees.

"Well done," the old man gasped as blood seeped between his fingers. Then the light went from his eyes, and he keeled over, falling headlong into the open grave to land on top of his wife's body.

"What the hell did you do that for?" Wade hissed as he looked down on them. But he knew, in his heart, that the old man wanted to join his wife in heaven and either lacked the courage to shoot himself or feared eternal damnation for doing it. Wade had been duped into providing the way out.

He stood at the graveside and said a silent prayer. He had to move quickly now. Even if the gunshots didn't attract the attention of a patrol, he had been delayed here when he should have found Becky by now.

But, sometimes, the human thing to do is not the rational choice.

So, he picked up the shovel and, as quickly as he could, he filled in the grave.

23

Elijah

In the end, Wade almost ran straight past the entrance to the high school, but then he spotted a glow emerging from the first-floor windows and halted to work out how to get in without being spotted.

The high school was within the protective cordon, but in an area that hadn't yet been declared entirely safe. He'd seen patrols making their noisy way through the streets here, looking for anyone out now that darkness had fallen, but they'd been easy enough to dodge. Any static guards on the entrances to the school would be tougher to get past.

He found a position on a low brick wall he could use to peer into the parking lot. Of course, none of the vehicles were moving, but most had escaped the night of the lights unscathed.

On impulse, he checked his arm again. "Jeez," he hissed. A barely perceptible glow reflected off his skin. He had no idea whether that meant he was receiving a dangerous dose, but he moved until he was under an overhang and waited a few minutes as the glow faded out entirely.

So, he guessed any irradiating lights hidden behind the clouds were pretty feeble. Perhaps they were receding? Maybe the Earth had traveled through some sort of band of radiation that was now going on to sterilize other worlds.

Pure speculation. For now, he kept himself under shelter and tried to work out where the guards were stationed.

After twenty minutes of impatient waiting, he'd identified a pair at the main entrance and a single guard at what was probably a fire escape. It was so damned dark now that the moon had vanished behind clouds, he couldn't be sure there weren't others, but he had no choice other than to move, and move quickly.

He would try the fire escape. He jumped down, aware that he was now out in the open and under whatever radiation was falling on him. But he couldn't wait any longer, so he ran, keeping low, across the parking lot, using cars and trucks as cover wherever possible.

When he'd made it a third of the way there, he saw someone move. Dropping to the floor, he got onto his knees and peered over the hood of a sedan. There was another guard he hadn't spotted before, making his way slowly around the school building's perimeter, heading toward the fire escape that was Wade's target.

He lowered his head as the guard got closer, pressing himself against the driver's window to keep out of sight. Then, as he looked along the side of the car, he saw out of his peripheral vision, someone looking back at him. He only just managed to swallow an exclamation that would surely have given him away. He was looking into the dead eyes of a middle-aged woman whose head was resting on the window, her fingers apparently clawing at the door, as if she'd been trapped inside when the pulse had struck and was too sick to get out.

What had humanity come to that this poor woman could have remained out here, unmissed, unnoticed, for days? How long would it be before anyone but Elijah Wade would find her? It reminded him of the COVID days when he would walk quiet streets totally unaware of the suffering going on behind closed doors. The city was like that — a Band-Aid of normality holding back the festering sore of coming chaos. He, and Becky, needed to be long gone by the time that happened.

He looked at the patch. The glow had intensified. He had to get inside, or he'd join the woman in the car. Keeping as low as he could, he scampered from car to car, getting closer to the fire-escape before stopping to reconnoiter again.

The second guard had joined the first. That made things much harder. He could handle one, but he was unlikely to be able to deal with two silently. His plan had been to subdue the guard without using lethal force — the man was probably a cop, after all — and then use his own cuffs to restrain him. But he couldn't see how he'd manage that when faced with two.

He'd have to try.

Then, one of the guards moved away until he had gone around the corner and Elijah could see the glow of a cigarette beneath a shelter of some sort. This was going to be his only chance.

He darted out from behind the nearest car, handgun extended and, by the time the guard had seen him, he was already so close that there was no chance for the man to even draw his weapon.

The guard put his hands up. Then he said, in an astonished voice, "Elijah? That you?"

"Joe? What the hell are you doing here?"

Sergeant Joe DeSantos wagged his finger. "No time for this. You got to get yourself out of here before Johnson comes back."

"I came for Becky. I won't go without her."

"Why not leave her here? Can't imagine anywhere safer."

Wade shook his head. "I promised to come back for her. Look, Joe, we were ambushed. McKinsey set us up. Killed Williams and most of the others."

"Jeez, Elijah, you just can't stay out of trouble, can you?"

"You don't sound surprised."

DeSantos looked toward the corner where his comrade was smoking. "We need a strong leader."

"We need a leader, not a mob boss."

"I'm sorry, Elijah, I really am." DeSantos snapped his weapon up before Wade could react. "Johnson, get over here at the double!"

"You son of a bitch. I guess you've chosen your side."

Wade heard swearing from behind him. "Where the hell did he come from? Who is he?"

"You shouldn't have come back," DeSantos said, taking Wade's 1911, then pushing the door open and guiding Wade into the half-light beyond. "Things have changed around here."

"They sure have."

DeSantos ignored Wade. "Cuff him."

As Johnson, a man half his age and, if he were any judge, half his brains, moved past DeSantos, and reached for his handcuffs he stumbled and cried out.

Wade took his chance. He brought his elbow up, connecting with Johnson's nose with a sickening crack and leaving the guard writhing on the floor, hands to his face.

DeSantos raised his sidearm, but he was slow, and Wade's backswing knocked it from his hands, sending it spinning across the floor. The sergeant seemed to overbalance, falling on his back as if he'd been pole axed. Wade picked DeSantos's gun from the floor and thrust it into his midriff.

"Elijah ..."

"Shut it. On your front."

The sergeant complied and Wade took out his cuffs and expertly fastened them one handed before going over to Johnson who was trying to groggily stem the blood-flow and repeating the exercise. "You're a dead man," Johnson said, spitting blood across the floor and Wade's jeans.

Wade pinned him with a knee in the back, then got up and kicked Johnson in the head before coming back to DeSantos. "You'd better hope you never see me again," he hissed before raising the sergeant's gun and pistol-whipping him across the head.

DeSantos slumped to the floor and Wade retrieved his 1911, then threw Johnson's weapon into a garbage can along the dark corridor before giving one final look at the carnage and running.

He had minutes at best. As soon as either of them regained consciousness, the call would go up and he'd be hunted like a rat.

Where could she be? The hall was at the center of most school layouts, and that would be as good a place as any to start his search, so he stumbled through the darkness, squinting up at barely visible signs until he finally emerged near the internal entrance.

How was he going to find her and get her out before the place was crawling with police? Then, as he passed a wall-mounted fire alarm, he had it. The oldest trick in the book. He smashed the alarm sensor with his elbow and, instantly the corridors filled with a weak oscillating siren powered by the battery backup.

Almost instantly, the dim shapes of people began emerging from ahead. He ran toward them, hands outstretched like a blind man, then plunged into an empty classroom, just in time to see the flow of people moving quickly past him.

Then, just as he was giving up hope, he saw her. She shrieked as he pulled her into the classroom, but none of the others tried to stop him, all focused on saving themselves from the fake fire.

"It's me!" he said, holding his hand over her mouth.

"Elijah? Oh my God! We've got to get out of here. There's a fire!"

"No, there isn't. But we do have to get out of here." He peered through the gap in the door. "That's the last of them. Come on!"

He grabbed her hand, and they ran along the corridor, past the school hall and into the darkness.

"Where are we going?"

"I don't know, but I want to find a way out on the other side of the building, as far from the main entrance as possible."

"Why are we running? I don't understand. Have you done something bad?"

"No. I don't have time to explain. You've got to trust me, okay?"

She mumbled an affirmative as they turned ninety degrees and continued through what looked like a science block; Wade could just make out lab benches through the open doors.

Then the fire alarm stopped, and the only sound was the echoing of their footsteps on the polished high school floor.

He could hear the sounds of voices calling, as if someone was organizing a hunt. And he knew who they were looking for. He felt like a cornered prey animal. Which way should he turn?

"Detective Elijah Wade!"

Someone was using a megaphone. It was hard to tell which direction the sound was coming from as it reflected off the hard walls.

"Detective Wade, you are surrounded. For your own sake, surrender and you will be taken without deadly force."

The implication was obvious. Give up or be shot like a dog.

"What did you do, Elijah?" Becky hissed.

"Survived. So far, anyway. McKinsey set a trap for me and the others. Sent us on a fake mission, then blew us up. I survived and one other. Now they want to finish what they started."

She looked up at him, eyes wide. For a moment, he thought she didn't believe him, but then she nodded. "What do we do?"

"Look, you should just hide here then make your way back to the hall and mingle with the others. No need for them to know you had anything to do with this."

"No way. You came back for me. I'd rather take my chances with you."

"That's crazy."

She shrugged. "Maybe you're right, but I don't care none. I'm coming with you and that's flat."

He led her into a classroom that had a fire door at the far end. They crouched beside a window that looked out onto the back of the parking lot.

"Dammit!" He could see distant shadows moving toward them, flashlights wandering back and forth as their pursuers searched for them. He'd hoped they'd be able to get out that way before they were encircled. "Look, Becky, I want you to hide here. There's no hope of getting away unnoticed."

"I said no, Elijah!"

"Don't you understand? This will have been for nothing if you get shot along with me. Now, do as you're told and let me go!"

He got up and ran for the door.

"Elijah!"

Without turning back, he burst through the fire escape and in that instant, the night was banished, then, moments later, a sound of thunder followed by a beating orange glow from the direction of the police department.

He felt Becky's hand in his. "Let's get out of here."

"The department's being attacked," he said, struggling to make sense of what he was seeing.

The silhouettes of their pursuers had turned and run toward headquarters as soon as they'd worked out what had happened.

"Then let's get away while we can," she said, pulling on his hand.

It didn't feel right. Even though they'd been hunting him, these were his colleagues. They'd been fed a lie about him, but they were fellow cops. And now they were fighting whoever had attacked the police department. Two bombs in one day — either McKinsey was behind them both, or whoever he'd employed to finish off Wade and the others had turned on him. So much for the strong man the city needed, according to DeSantos, at least.

As he ran into the fire-tinged darkness, he thought of all he was leaving behind. A lifetime of service and duty. And at what cost? A marriage, a functioning relationship with his daughter, and now every friend he'd ever had. Even Joe DeSantos.

He used the flickering amber glow to navigate their way. And he finally realized, deep in his soul, that everything he'd known, everything he'd held important, was gone and would never come back. All he had was the promises he'd made.

One was to Becky, that, having rescued her from a monster, he would protect her.

And the overriding promise to his daughter. He would escape the city and begin the long journey to find her. "Kelly," he whispered, "I'm coming."

24

Grace

Day 4: Southern Texas

Walter drifted in and out of consciousness as Grace sat in an old dining chair she'd dragged up to the bedroom and tried to stay awake. Night had fallen, and aside from the irregular breathing noises her husband was making, all she could hear was the rain hitting the back of the house.

She sat in the darkness, the flickering light of a candle playing over her husband's face and prayed for him. Truth was, she'd thought about walking out on him a thousand times over the past years. She didn't like him much, and he'd barely shown a scrap of love to her since they were married. Oh, he'd worked hard and provided for the family, sure, but he'd never been capable of the sort of love she needed: the kind you see in those Hallmark movies. Some people had that kind of relationship with their husband, but not her.

But, she was self-aware enough to know that movies aren't real life, and she'd never done anything about leaving him. First, when Lyle was a baby, she couldn't have managed on her own. And then it seemed too late. And, anyway, she'd played her part in bringing their son into the world, she needed to provide a stable home for him. Though, given how he'd turned out, maybe she'd have been better off running for the hills long ago. Maybe right about the time Lyle came home with that upside down crucifix tattooed onto his foot.

Now, as her husband lay there, grievously ill, she found that she did care about him. She didn't want him to go —

and not only for the practical reason that the world was turning upside down and she was scared of being a woman on her own. They hadn't loved each other in any romantic sense, but they'd grown together like two trees planted beside each other that merge into one over time.

No, she had to have faith that he would pull through and they could experience the Rapture together, though how they could be happy in Heaven while their son was consumed by flame, she couldn't imagine.

"Gracie."

She snapped out of her slumber and leaned forward.

"Give me some more meds."

"No, Walt. It might kill you."

His head rolled back and forth on the pillow. "I don't care. Get me some Jim Beam, will ya?"

She looked into his desperate eyes, sighed and went downstairs to fetch the bourbon. She'd half hoped he'd be asleep by the time she returned, but he was lying there, looking up at her, the pain and desperation obvious. The redness on his face had become deeper and was now mixing with black bruising that was spreading up from around his neck. She hoped this was a sign of healing but knew in her heart it wasn't.

"Here, but just a little, mind," she said, pouring a measure into his favorite glass. She put a hand under his head to tilt him upwards and held the glass to his lips with the other. But as he opened his mouth, he pushed at her, taking a mouthful and swallowing.

"Another."

"Walter!"

"Do as I say, woman!"

She could have ignored him, take the bottle away and shut the door. But then he'd try to get up and she'd have to lift him back to the bed when he fell. With all the meds he'd had, he'd struggle to put one foot in front of the other even if he was stone cold sober.

And, after all, who was she to refuse him? He wasn't a child, though he sure acted like one often enough.

"Okay. But take it slower this time."

He did, but the second glass was soon empty.

"Now, go to bed, Gracie. Get some sleep. I'll be okay."

She leaned forward to ask him if he was sure, but he'd fallen asleep.

Grace woke to the sound of a dog barking. After a moment's confusion, she realized it was Boomer. He had free rein from his kennel near the house's front door right up to the wire fence that linked with the road outside, and he was barking his lungs out. Opening the drapes, she couldn't see anything, but it was late, and the earlier gentle rainfall had turned into a torrent.

She pulled the Savage 24 rifle from its place in the frayed easy chair she'd used to nurse Lyle all those years ago, back when she'd imagined a world of possibilities in front of him, none of which involved a jail cell. Once she'd realized that Walter wasn't getting up anytime soon, she'd retrieved it from the armory and kept it close. Cracking the rifle open, she ran her fingers over both chambers, checking they were loaded, then shut the rifle and pushed the selector down to choose the 410. "No time for pussy-footing around, Gracie," she muttered to herself. She kept her combination rifle nearby whenever she was outside and brought it upstairs at bedtime. She'd only fired it in anger a couple of times, and only ever at animals, but she was a woman on her own right now, with Walter dosed up on meds, and she felt a whole lot more comfortable with a shotgun shell locked and loaded.

Running one hand down the wall, she made her way slowly down the stairs, wondering whether she was more likely to break her neck in the darkness than she was to come to harm from whomever, or whatever, was out there. But this was the procedure, and even though Walter wasn't awake to check on her, she was going to stick to it.

She shook her head to clear her thoughts. That was her problem — always going down rabbit holes when she really needed to focus on what was in front of her. Her mind was like a hamster in a wheel ... and there, she'd done it again.

Boomer was still barking, and she could hear his rope rubbing on the side of the house. He sure was trying to get to whoever was out there. She found the door of their situation room — really nothing more than a broom cupboard, but Walter liked to pretend he was still in the military. She activated the CCTV monitor that covered the front gate, squinting up at the black and white infrared image. There was Boomer and, beyond him, a dark, indistinct, shape leaning against the bars. She couldn't see it moving and it didn't look threatening to her, but she had to be careful.

She returned to the hallway that led to the front door and pulled on her coat and a baseball cap. The intruder had to be desperate to be out at night, in weather like this. There was no way of knowing whether the lights were in the sky, above the rain. Or whether they could penetrate the cloud cover if they were. But she wouldn't take the risk. Boomer was smart enough to keep under cover when they were there, perhaps by some animal instinct or sense that humans didn't possess.

As she stood by the front door, Grace glanced over her shoulder, seeing that all the lights in the house were off, and slipped into the dark. She felt the cool drips of water running down her face as she half-tip-toed her way along the driveway, keeping to the edge, looking out of the corners of her eyes to help her follow the line of thorny bushes that marked where the gravel gave way to scrubby grass. A cool wind rustled the wet leaves like the whisper of death.

"Help!"

She froze as she heard the voice. It was a woman. Young. She relaxed a little, noticing for the first time her fingers cramping around the rifle.

"Please. Please help me..."

Grace knew she couldn't be seen as she edged forward, so the woman was calling out in a desperation that even Boomer seemed to have understood as he'd stopped barking. She patted the dog's head as he snuggled into her legs, keeping slightly ahead of her, still primed for attack.

And then she heard the unmistakable sound of a baby crying.

Again, she stopped, feeling the hand of destiny on her shoulder, a deep dread filling her insides with ice.

But Boomer nudged her, licking her unburdened hand, urging her forward.

So, she began moving again until a flashlight snapped on from the other side of the gate, darting around like a searchlight until, finally, it reached Grace who put her hand up to shield her eyes.

"Oh, thank God. Please ... help me." The woman stood on the other side of the gate, with something silver-colored wrapped around her.

Grace walked quickly forward until she was at the gate's bars. She turned on her Maglite and swept it left and right, looking for anyone else beside the woman who'd been calling and finding no one.

"What do you want?" Grace asked, peering at the face beyond the bars.

She was a young woman — mid-twenties, Grace guessed — but she looked as sick as hell. The light brown skin of her face was violated by red wheals, making her look like a victim of bubonic plague or a zombie apocalypse. Grace sighed and shook her head.

"I'm sick," the young woman said.

"I'm sorry to hear that, but I'm no doctor. I got some meds you can have ..."

The woman shook her head. "Too late." She unfolded the silver shawl she'd wrapped around herself, and Grace caught sight of a dark, wrinkly face.

"Heavens, baby looks barely full baked!"

"She was born a week ago. I ... I was in an ambulance ... going home. The driver ... got sick."

Grace shook her head. "How long you been walking, sweetheart?"

A shrug. "Hours. Tried to get under cover when I heard that sound — you know, like singing. Comes when the lights are in the sky. Thought this foil might protect a little, but I got sick anyway."

Then, quite suddenly, she slumped against the bars and slid to the ground, still clutching the baby to her chest.

Grace unlocked and pulled the gate open as Boomer bounded past her to run up and down, looking for intruders before returning to where the woman lay.

Rolling her onto her back, Grace stroked the ruined face. "What's your name, darlin'?"

The eyes opened for a moment, looking directly into Grace's as the old woman's tears began to fall, mixing with the rain. "Hope ..." she said. And, with that, she went still.

"What did you say?" But there was no answer.

Grace looked up at the night sky, wiping away at her face, and asked Jesus what she should do.

"I can't do it, Lord!" she cried out, rain falling into her open mouth. "Walter's deathly sick, and Lyle's missing. I buried a friend yesterday. You know that! Why did you bring this child to me? I got to look after my husband! I got to look after Walter."

She let the cap fall from her head as she kneeled on the wet asphalt, desperately hoping to perceive the voice of wisdom from on high.

She didn't hear any actual words. But, as she kneeled there in the wet, she knew what she had to do, as sure as the rain was falling. There was purpose in this, and she had to have enough faith to try to do the right thing, and that she'd find the strength to do it.

Gently, she prized the woman's arms apart and lifted the baby out of its mother's embrace. She took the bundle inside the gate, putting it down in a concrete flower trough, and ordering Boomer to guard it. Then she took the small pack from the woman's shoulder and pulled her body inside to keep it from the coyotes before covering it in the silver foil. She'd deal with it tomorrow.

She did all this in a numb, robotic manner, one step at a time, her mind closed off to the significance and grief of what had just happened.

But the pungent stench that assaulted her nose as she lifted the baby out of the flower trough snapped her back to reality. The child bawled, mouth wide open, as water began to seep through its coat.

"Our Lord and Savior," she muttered. "Let's get you inside." She held the child at arm's length and headed toward the house. She turned as she reached the door, unable to see where the mother lay. Then she looked up. The rain had stopped, and the sky was clearing. Tenuous threads of color pulsed in the heavens, growing stronger as she watched. And the air sang.

She hurried into the house, shutting the door and immediately unwrapping the child before setting it down on the couch where Brandan had been. "So, you're a girl," she said, as she found the diapers in the woman's pack.

Once she'd pulled off her rain-soaked coat and kicked away her boots, she kneeled beside the child and removed the old diaper. "Lord, but I'd forgotten that smell," she said, wrinkling her nose. As she worked, she tried to focus on the practical and the short term. There was a small can of infant formula in the pack, and a change of clothes, but she'd need more soon enough. She'd call Rita in the morning. Their community was all well past child-bearing age, but some of them had had grandchildren, or great grandchildren, in the past few years, so maybe they'd have some spares. If not, she'd just have to make do. The diapers she could manage without, at a pinch, and she had dried milk powder in the basement — though it wasn't near nutritious enough for a young baby. She could probably make something for the child to wear out of one of Walter's T-shirts. Yes, one way or another, she'd manage the practicalities. Plenty of children had been born into worse conditions than this little one. Our Lord, for one.

She went into the kitchen and made up the infant formula with some cool water from the kettle, then settled back on the couch, looking down at the baby as she guzzled the milk.

Then, as she felt that surge of joy and relief that comes when a baby is feeding, she noticed that tears were falling onto the child.

Tears of grief for the losses she'd already suffered and those that were inevitably coming. Tears of fear for an unknowable future. And tears of happiness and relief because, as she fed this baby, she knew that, at least for now, she'd found her purpose. She would do her duty by Walter, and help him recover, if that was God's will, but she had discovered a greater responsibility. She would protect this child with her life.

Grace looked down at the baby as she finished the bottle and drifted off. "Now, you need to have a name. What did your mommy say, right before she passed? I asked what she was called."

Grace thought back to the last moments of the child's mother. She'd uttered one word — it might have been her name, or it could have been simply the start of a sentence she never finished. But, either way, it would do for now.

"Sleep well, my little one," Grace said, the world consisting of nothing but her and the child in that moment. "You are my Hope."

Epilogue

Day 1, Glendale, CA

Silas Lynch sat in the pen with the flashlight on his lap, listening to the sounds of a city dying, and smiling. He switched the flashlight off and began his count to one hundred. One hundred seconds with the light on, one hundred with the light off. That way, he doubled the life of the battery. He shouldn't have to do it — the cop had promised to come back, but he guessed all bets were off now. And he didn't forgive Wade.

Of course, he knew the name of the detective leading the hunt for him. Silas wasn't your common or garden serial killer. He was an artist. He took pride in his craft. And he was so fastidious — removing every trace of the victim from the scene of their murder — that they'd named him the Cleaner. But he must have slipped up somewhere, otherwise how had Wade caught up with him just as things had begun to get interesting. He was on his way home to drug Molly and use the truck to take her to a new location. He named each of his victims after a famous prostitute. It robbed them of identity as he robbed them of breath.

99, 100.

Silas examined his hands in the flashlight beam and began picking away at the tiny traces of blood still under his fingernails. He should have worn gloves. Foolish, foolish.

If only he hadn't been caught just as the city was falling apart. What fun he could have had. It was obvious to him that the illness and madness was caused by the aurora. He'd heard, and felt, some sort of impact that he guessed was a plane crashing.

Grinding his teeth, he got up and wrapped his fingers around the bars, staring at the door that led to the sergeant's desk.

Then he heard shouting. Closer, this time. Glass smashed beyond the door, and the distinctive voices of police trying to exert control and failing.

The smell of burning.

They were petrol-bombing the police station! When he'd been delighting in the destruction of the city, he hadn't imagined he'd be trapped here, helpless to either take part or escape.

The door to the sergeant's desk swung open and a silhouette looked in at him.

"Get me out of here!" Silas shouted. He was really beginning to panic now. He hated confined spaces at the best of times, but he could smell burning plastic and knew that if he didn't get out, he'd likely be burned alive.

The figure looked over its shoulder, yelled, "Roast in hell," and slammed the door.

Silas yelled at the top of his voice, but all he could hear beyond the door was the sound of the police station being wrecked, and voices shouting in delight.

In the end, he slid down the bars and lay sobbing on the floor.

He didn't know how long he sat there, by turns raging and crying, but he could barely breathe by the time the door opened again.

"Help me!"

Figures stood there, silhouetted against the amber flickering of flames.

"There ain't nothin' in here. Just the jail," one figure shouted above the crackling of the fire. "C'mon, let's go."

"Help!!" Silas yelled.

A slim shape detached itself from the others, but the first speaker called to him. "What you doin'? We gotta get our asses outta here! Leave him be!"

But the slim figure moved toward the bars. "You go on!" He didn't look behind as the others vanished.

"What you in here for?"

"Dealer ratted me out," Silas said, snatching the first idea that came into his head.

"Fosho?" It was a young Black man, carrying a knife. He looked at Silas for a moment, then nodded. "Where are the keys?"

"I don't know. I saw the sergeant come out of there."

The young man ran into the office as Silas waited, gripping the bars in sweaty hands. He coughed and put tried to breathe through his sleeve, but he wouldn't last long. And the air was getting hot.

"Got them!" His rescuer began trying each key one at a time. "Bad enough to be shut up like a animal. But to be left to burn to death..."

"I appreciate it," Silas said as the key finally turned, and the door swung open.

"Now, you follow me, and I'll show you the safe ..."

Silas reached out, grabbed the young man's knife and plunged it into his chest before pulling it out again. He fell like a sack of bricks, and Silas grabbed him by the boots and dragged him into the cell. He left the flashlight there, slammed the door shut and, for a final theatrical flourish, wrapped the young man's hands around the bars as if he'd been trying to escape.

He wiped the blade on a police jacket and opened the door to the outer office. Heat blasted his face, but he could see a path between the flames that would take him outside. He hoped he wouldn't run into his rescuer's friends but, if he did, he'd deal with them as well.

Silas ran for it, the heat burning his arms and legs from both sides. He felt his hair ignite and he roared in pain as he tripped, falling face down in the hot detritus. Pulling himself up, he leaped for the door and emerged, his clothes on fire, into the night where, mercifully, a cold, gentle rain was falling. From nowhere, the thought struck him that he must have looked like the human torch to anyone watching. But no one moved, so he dragged himself up out of the wet and slipped into the night.

He would find somewhere to hide. Not his apartment. Wade was sure to go there, and Silas was too weak from his wounds to face him just yet. Silas had been lucky — that young man had appeared just in time. People with a conscience were so useful, so easy to manipulate. Their great flaw was to believe the lie that you should do to others what you would have them do to you. He could have let his rescuer go, but he knew Wade might return, and that he'd check on the cells, expecting to see a charred body there. And now he would find one.

Silas would hole up, nurse his wounds — or find someone to nurse them for him — and, when he was well again, he would go after Wade. Chances were he'd stay in Glendale to help out, but if not, Silas would find someone who knew where he'd gone. That sergeant, for example, the one who'd left him to burn. Oh, yes. Silas would make him pay for that.

And once he knew where to find Elijah Wade, no power on heaven or Earth would stop him. He would take his revenge on Wade and get him to tell Silas where Moll was. Then he would find her and finish the job. And, finally, he would be able to wash his hands clean.

***

Get   the   next   book   here! (books2read.com/nightfallseries2)

Aftermath: Book 2 of the Nightfall Series

After a beautiful but deadly lightshow, humanity is on the brink of extinction. And in the midst of this chaos, the ruthless will be king.

Author's Note

I'm a science geek, I won't deny it. So, I like the sci-fi I write to be as founded in realism as possible, while giving myself the necessary leeway to serve the creative needs of the story.

Believe it or not, the genesis of this story was an account I came upon of Captain James Cook's expedition to observe the transit of the planet Venus in 1761. I was intrigued by the controversy that surrounded the expedition and the castigation of the official astronomer, Charles Green, who died on the return journey. He took the blame for the inaccuracy of the measurements (even though Cook himself made separate records which were also inaccurate) and I wondered whether, just possibly, he'd spotted something in the sky that was later expunged from the records. This becomes particularly relevant in book 2 of the series when Hannah recovers a mysterious journal from the Russian observatory.

So, I wanted a somewhat plausible apocalyptic event with a scientific explanation (which Hannah, our astronomer, will discover over the course of the series with devastating consequences) that also scratched my research itch while being an ongoing threat to the survivors.

I then assembled a varied cast, each with a different view of what's happening, from a non-religious scientist to a believer in the end times who sees her beliefs being fulfilled. And in the middle of it all there's our main protagonist, Elijah Wade, who now realizes that his decades-long devotion to his career came at too high a cost. He will stop at nothing in his search for redemption.

My stories have, at their core, the belief that ordinary people can do extraordinary things when push comes to shove. These books, like all my novels, focus on examining what it is to be human in the most extreme circumstances. And, despite their post-apocalyptic setting, they're all hopeful tales with, ultimately, a positive message.

Kev Partner

Free Story and More from Me

Fancy a free post apocalyptic story? Click here to download Final Justice (https://scrib.me/finaljustice), the first appearance of John Hunter, judge, jury and executioner.

And here's where you can find more from me:

Website: www.kevpartner.co.uk

Library: books2read.com/rl/kevpartner

Follow me on Bookbub: www.bookbub.com/authors/kevin-partner

Facebook: www.fb.com/KevPartnerAuthor

Printed in Great Britain
by Amazon